"Kristin McKaslin, is that you?"

Kristin studied the man who sank into the empty seat across the aisle. He was good-looking, with disheveled black hair and eyes a sharp aquamarine-blue. The straight blade of a nose, high cheekbones, a simple cut into his chin.

Nope, she didn't know him, but there was something familiar about him. She didn't know him from work. Or the gym. Or church. Either in Seattle or Montana... Wait. There was something distinctive about that devastating smile. Those dimples, and that strong jaw.

Then she knew. She saw a flash of a boyish face with longer black hair standing before the podium at a high school assembly. The image of a leaner, younger star running back, whipping off his helmet after the final touchdown of the state championship. The studious salutatorian-to-be ambling down the hall and stopping to open the door to physics class for her.

"Ryan Sanders?" She couldn't believe it.

Books by Jillian Hart

Love Inspired

Heaven Sent #143
*His Hometown Girl #180
A Love Worth Waiting For #203
Heaven Knows #212
*The Sweetest Gift #243
*Heart and Soul #251
*Almost Heaven #260
*Holiday Homecoming #272

*The McKaslin Clan

JILLIAN HART

makes her home in Washington State, where she has lived most of her life. When Jillian is not hard at work on her next story, she loves to read, go to lunch with her friends and spend quiet evenings with her family.

HOLIDAY
HOMECOMING

JILLIAN HART

Steeple
Hill®

Published by Steeple Hill Books™

STEEPLE HILL BOOKS

Steeple Hill®

ISBN 0-373-87282-8

HOLIDAY HOMECOMING

www.SteepleHill.com

Printed in U.S.A.

These are the things that will endure—faith, hope, and love—and the greatest of these is love.
—1 *Corinthians* 13:13

Chapter One

November 23

Disaster.

Kristin McKaslin took one look at the snow-caked airplane window and groaned. She was doomed. That window had been only a little bit icy less than twenty minutes ago, when she'd looked up from her work. Now she couldn't see through it, not that there was anything to see at this altitude and with the plane swinging in the turbulence.

At least it gave her something to think about other than heading home to Montana. Thanksgiving was tomorrow, and that was both good and bad. She loved her sisters. She loved her parents. She loved going home to visit.

What she wasn't looking forward to was facing her mother's disappointments. She lived too far away. She didn't come home to visit enough. She wasn't married.

And she wasn't married. Mom was doubly unhappy about that one.

Just because she wasn't married, it didn't mean she was a failure, right?

Right. So, why did it feel that way? And why was it such a big deal? A marriage certificate came with no guarantees, and as far as she could tell, it didn't protect a person against heartbreak, disappointment and loneliness.

It wasn't as if Mom and Dad were ecstatic in their nearly forty years of marriage. But it wasn't as if she could say that to Mom. She hated pretending, as if nothing had changed in their family, when everything had.

That was the real reason she didn't want to walk through the front door of her childhood home. It was too painful to think about.

"Kristin McKaslin, is that you?"

She studied the well-dressed man who sank into the empty seat across the aisle. He was good-looking with disheveled black hair and eyes a sharp aquamarine blue. He had a straight blade of a nose, high cheekbones and dimples cut into his cheeks. He was dressed in a casual outfit that shouted, "Money!"

Nope, she didn't know him, but wait, there *was* something familiar about him. But what?

She didn't know him from work, the gym or church—either in Seattle or in Montana. Still, there was *something* distinctive about that devastating smile, those dimples…and that strong jaw.

Of course! She saw a flash of a boyish face with longer black hair standing before the podium at a high-school assembly. The image of a leaner, younger star running back whipping off his helmet after the final touchdown for the state championship. The caustic face of her mom's best friend's son, who wanted to be anywhere but stuck waiting in the car while their mothers talked on the sidewalk in town.

"Ryan Sanders?" She couldn't believe it. She blinked, and the remembered youthful image of his face blended with the older, wiser one staring back at her across the aisle. "It *is* you."

"The one and only. I look different, I know, everybody says so. I went and got respectable."

"You were always respectable."

"Nope, I wasn't. You're just being nice." His cute lopsided grin had matured into a slow curve of a smile. "You look better, but the same. Still have your nose in a book."

"Guilty. I confess."

Those blue eyes, which could have been cold, sparkled. "That's how I recognized you."

"I'm surprised you could see me over the seats. I'm still short."

"The word is 'petite.' I was bored and people-watching and I could see your profile from way back there. I got the last seat on the plane I think."

"Waited until the last minute?"

"I didn't think I'd be flying out of Seattle. Hey, you cut your hair. It was always long. Hiding your face. It still does, even short." He reached across the aisle to touch the curled end of her chin-length hair.

She felt a jolt, like the snap of static shock, as the lock of hair rebounded against her jaw. What was that? And should she act as if she *hadn't* felt it? "Your hair's shorter, too."

"It goes with my more reputable image." He shrugged one dependable shoulder.

Yeah, he looked reputable, all right, decked out in a loose-knit black sweater that hugged the lean curves of his muscled shoulders and chest. Black trousers, crisply pleated, completed the image.

He could be a corporate heavyweight, with a stuffy MBA and an impressive portfolio. Except for the black boots, scuffed and rugged, showing there was still a part of the Montana boy in the polished, educated man.

He raked his hand through his short, unruly black locks and leaned into the corner of the seat. A big powerful man, sprawled out like a kid, his large feet crossed at the ankles in the aisle.

"So, what's a pretty girl like you doing with a laptop and a book at—" he glanced at the gold flash of his Rolex "—9:07 at night?"

"Working."

"Yeah? I remembered you were studious in high school. What did the valedictorian of Valley High grow up to be?"

"An advertising executive."

"Well done. You live in Seattle?"

"I do. Not a hard guess, since the flight originated there. You, too?"

"Nope, just up checking out a job offer." Less comfortable talking about that, he hauled his feet in from the aisle and sat up straight. Too late to change the subject. It wasn't pretty Kristin McKaslin's fault his life was messed up.

Okay, it wasn't a mess *yet,* but it wasn't the fit he wanted, either. He'd become a successful doctor. It just didn't feel right to him. And after the breakup with Francine—

"Wow, a job offer." Kristin was even prettier when she smiled. "Who in their right mind would hire you?"

"Right. I'm suspicious of their offer right up front." They'd been good people, that's what. Professional, smart, with a good, positive focus. Not at all like the profit-oriented outfit he was stuck with in Scottsdale. "What kind of dudes are they, if they want me to join up with 'em?"

"Smart ones. Are you gonna go for it?"

A loaded question, but his problems weren't Kristin's, so he'd leave out the personal stuff. "Not sure about what I'm gonna do. I'm looking for a change. I have a great practice, but Phoenix is a little hot for me in the summers. Still, I suppose that's why air-conditioning was invented."

"Your practice? Oh, wait. I remember something about you getting into medical school long ago. Knowing you, that *couldn't* be true."

"Hard to believe they actually took a no-account like me."

"For a jock, you weren't *too* dumb. Guess how hard I had to study to beat your GPA?"

"Hard? Good, cuz I worked my toes off and I couldn't get half as many one hundred percents as you did."

She sparkled, but not in the way of women who realized he was a single man *and* a doctor. No, she was quiet class, all the way from her polished brown loafers to the carefully folded neck of her sort-of-brown turtleneck. Warm, though, not stuffy.

Her voice was soft elegance. "What kind of doctor are you?"

"An orthopedic surgeon."

"Sure, you have the ego for it."

"Hey, I don't deserve that. Okay, maybe I do. But I like helping people. Fixing their blown-out knees and torn ankles. What about you? An advertising exec, huh? Does that mean you're a big shot in the advertising world?"

"Yeah, right. I make sure the agency runs without a hitch. It's a good job but not very glamorous."

"I can see you, diligent and kind and handling everything just right."

"Same old Ryan, charming and full of it. Some things never change."

"Don't they? Back in school you were too high and mighty for me."

"High and mighty?"

"One of the perfect McKaslin girls."

"Perfect, my foot! Good grief, I'm a mess. A walking disaster."

"Yeah, uh-huh. You sure look like it." He rolled his eyes to emphasize his point. Ryan didn't think there could be a nicer family of women on the planet.

Part of the McKaslin genes, he figured. With Kristin, there was no mistaking her girl-next-door freshness, even in her power suit.

What kind of executive did she make? One who said please and thank-you, was his guess, and it clashed with the ice-princess high-end designer jacket, sweater and slacks she wore.

Maybe he'd lived in a big city for too long. Whoa— that thought was something his mom would say. Not for the first time tonight he wished he'd paid for his mom to come down for Thanksgiving. Montana came with too many lessons learned. Lessons that haunted him to this day.

"It's weird seeing you like this. On the same plane heading home." It blew his mind, that's what, because he didn't believe in coincidences. All things happened for a reason.

"I haven't seen you since, what, high school?"

"When I left for college, I left for good. I keep trying to lure Mom to Phoenix, but she won't do it. She calls every Sunday afternoon, after church. To make sure I've gone to worship like a good son."

"Good. You need someone to keep you in line. I've lost track of nearly everyone. It's weird how in school we had all the time in the world, our future ahead of us, and now that we're in the middle of those futures, there's no time at all."

"Exactly. Now I put in long hours. I've got no time."

"What? You're a doctor. Why are you working long days? Don't you people golf on Tuesdays and Fridays?"

"Some do. I have school loans to make good on, and the balance is higher than most people's mortgages."

"Ouch. I'm glad I worked my way through school."

He crooked a doubtful eyebrow. "Worked? Didn't you get the only four-year scholarship in our graduating class?"

"Yeah, but that was for tuition. I had a part-time job in the university library on the weekends, and I worked during the summers."

"I was volunteering in clinics and did a year in the Peace Corps so I had a better shot at med school."

"I've heard medical school isn't all that competitive."

That made him laugh. "Yeah. I spent a year in the Dominican Republic assisting a physician. That year did more to make a man of me than anything. I hope it made me a much better doctor."

"I can't imagine you're a bad one. Arrogant, maybe."

"Hey!" He laughed with her. He liked her, he couldn't help it. But seeing her reminded him of a time in his life that was complicated. "It's good to see you. I'm glad you're doing well."

"You, too." Kristin closed the laptop and focused her full attention on Ryan Sanders. Dr. Ryan Sanders. That was going to take some getting used to. She could still see the spirited young boy inside the responsible man.

Not that she was interested. So she'd noticed that his

left hand was suntanned and ringless. He'd made the effort of renewing their acquaintance. He'd been so complimentary and friendly. Why was she even thinking in this direction?

Doom. Disaster. She'd never wanted a relationship. She would never lean on a man. She was fine all by herself, even if that got lonely sometimes.

"Here comes the beverage cart. I'd better get back to my seat now or I'll be trapped here." He rose, all six feet plus of him, filling the aisle. "Maybe I'll see you around town?"

"Maybe. If I see you on the sidewalk, I won't run in the opposite direction."

"Deal. I'll try not to run into a store and hide from ya."

And he was gone, ambling down the aisle.

Ryan Sanders. He filled her thoughts as she opened the three-ring binder and flipped up the laptop's screen. Imagine that, running into him. Had she even heard much about Ryan over the years?

No, just comments from Mom now and then on how Mary's son had straightened out his life. Finally. And how Mary was lonely for him.

Wasn't loneliness an integral part of life? Troubled, Kristin tried to concentrate on the Myers budget and couldn't. The numbers on the screen fuzzed, and she rubbed her tired eyes.

Father, I don't want to go home. Guilt warred with the other emotions coiling up in her stomach. *What do I do?*

She couldn't disappoint her mom. Mom had been

pressuring her since Labor Day, to make sure Kristin would come home. What did you do when home was no longer a refuge? A place that hurt instead of sheltered?

A sharp pain slashed like a razor in her stomach and had her digging through her bag for the roll of antacids she ate like candy. She loved her parents. She loved her sisters.

But all her girlhood illusions of family had died along with Allison. Time had not mended the broken places in her heart or in her family.

How could she go home and pretend nothing was wrong?

She *wanted* to see her sisters. Hold her newest niece, Anna, who'd been born in late summer. Gramma would be there. She wanted to see her parents.

If only there was a way to come home without the pain and sadness…

The plane dipped sharply to the left, and fear shattered her thoughts. She gripped the armrest. Was her heart really beating that fast? She took a deep breath, her chest pounding. What was wrong? She *hated* flying. Absolutely hated it.

What if it was engine trouble? Ice had crusted over the little window next to her. What if there was a problem with ice or something? She tried not to think of horror stories of air disasters. *This* was how Allison had died, in a plane crash in bad weather.

"Attention, passengers, this is your captain speaking."

Kristin's ears popped. Were they losing altitude? Before she could unscramble her thoughts to pray, the pilot continued speaking. "There's a blizzard in Missoula so we're diverting to Boise International."

A blizzard? That was all? They weren't going to crash? Relief slid through her like ice water. *Thank you, Lord.* She clutched the small cross at her neck. That was the good news, but a blizzard? What blizzard?

Sure, it was snowing, but the weatherpeople had promised the snow would be light. Okay, so it wouldn't be the first time a weatherman was wrong, and this *was* Montana. Extreme weather happened. But Boise?

Going home might not be the easiest thing, but she missed her sisters. She didn't want to spend Thanksgiving alone.

See? She would have been better off driving, with snow forecasted or not! There was that Murphy's Law in effect again. Whatever would turn out worse, she had a habit of picking it.

This will work out for the best. She took a deep breath, willed her tensed muscles to unclench just a little. *Right, Lord?*

Right. Everything happened as it was meant to be. So this was simply a safer route than if she'd driven over the pass and right into the blizzard. By going to Boise, they were going around the storm. It made sense.

She'd just catch a flight when she got to Boise. Surely there would be a few vacant seats somewhere on a late-night flight to Bozeman.

And if not, she'd just rent a car and drive. The blizzard was in the other direction, right?

Thanksgiving

Wrong. The flights had been canceled. The Boise airport was closing down due to the rapidly approaching surprise storm. The blizzard was bringing dangerous conditions to half the cities in northern Idaho and to all of midwestern Montana.

Great. And if that wasn't bad enough, there wasn't a car left to rent in all of Boise. Kristin ought to know. She'd called every place that would answer their phone at 12:06 on Thanksgiving morning.

There were no hotel vacancies, no motel vacancies and the local bed-and-breakfasts weren't picking up.

Definitely a problem. Kristin buttoned her coat and stared at her reflection in the black windows of the airport terminal. What was she going to do? Fat chunks of snow floated to the white ground on the other side of the glass where a single taxi waited along a vacant curb.

No passengers rushed from baggage claim or hurried to make that last-minute flight. She was practically alone and the security guards were eyeing her suspiciously. The swish of a janitor's wide mop seemed loud in the echoing silence.

It looked as if she would miss Thanksgiving at home.

No sisters. No baby niece to hug close. No roasted turkey with Gramma's special stuffing.

On the other hand, she wouldn't have to face Allison's empty place at the table.

But not seeing *any* of her sisters… Her chest ached

with sadness. How could she be sad at completely opposite things at once?

So, she'd spend this holiday alone. She lived alone. She spent lots of weekends alone. She was used to it.

Still, loneliness grabbed hard and squeezed. For as much as she dreaded some things, she missed others very much. The way Mom always greeted her at the door, wearing her apron and opening her arms wide for a hug.

The big country kitchen would be warm with the delicious fragrances of roasting turkey and baking bread and desserts set out to cool on the counter.

Her sisters laughing and quibbling while her nieces and nephew toddled around the living room, and everyone turning to shout, "It's Kristin. Kristin's here!"

Exhausted from starting work at six o'clock this morning so she could leave early for the airport, she was too tired even to pray. Aching with despair, she buried her face in her hands.

Chapter Two

If that wasn't a sign from above, Ryan didn't know what was. He'd stood in line at one car-rental place after another. No rental cars. The passengers had dispersed; he detoured to baggage claim and was stunned to see his suitcase circling. He had the worst luck *ever* when it came to airport baggage.

Yup, it was a sign. This attempted trip home wasn't over yet. Okay, he was going to give the rental counters one more try. If there were no cars, then he'd done all he could. It looked as if he *wouldn't* be going home for Thanksgiving.

But he couldn't be that lucky. He was probably the only human being on the continent who was hoping to head *away* from home.

Of course, there was a last-minute cancellation and an SUV with four-wheel drive just happened to be available—the only car left for rent in the entire city. Providence had spoken. Ryan Sanders was going to spend

Thanksgiving with his family. No excuses, no exceptions. He might as well accept it and make the best of it.

It would mean a lot to Mom. That's what mattered, at least telling himself that gave him enough grit to accept his fate. He loved his mom, he loved his sister, but he didn't miss Montana. He wanted to put that part of his life away and lock the door tight. Throw the key in a deep well and cover it up. For good. There were some places too painful to go, like the past.

That's why he believed in going full steam ahead. Why he never looked back. Why he wasn't thrilled as he loaded up the Jeep and flipped the defroster on high. The Good Lord was making His will pretty clear in spite of the weather. The snowstorm was working up into a blizzard on the other side of the snowy windshield. The wipers couldn't keep up.

Great, how was he going to see where he was going? Ryan squinted into the dizzying downfall but it didn't help. He couldn't read the directional signs through the whiteout conditions. Should he go left or right?

Clueless, he went left. He barely touched the brake and the tires did a little skid on the ice. Talk about dangerous conditions. He was a decent driver, but there was no sense in putting himself or anyone else at risk. A fair amount of his practice was comprised of car-accident victims. He'd done enough rotation time in the E.R. to know what could happen.

Maybe the wisest thing to do was hunt down a hotel room *somewhere*. Boise was crammed full of stranded travelers who'd booked every available room for the holiday weekend. He knew because he'd spent forty straight minutes on the phone. But maybe there was something available farther down the road, in one of the little towns a few miles north. He'd drive until he found a motel room—he wasn't picky. He was too tired to drive on icy highways until dawn.

Okay, where had the road gone? It had to be somewhere in front of him. There was a metal post, good thing he didn't hit it. Wait—a soft glow of light broke through the blizzard.

Perfect. He was headed the wrong way. The snow thinned on the lee side of the terminal as he crept through the empty passenger-loading zone. There was only a lonely taxi waiting alongside the curb with lights blinking. It was quickly being covered by snowfall.

Light from the terminal broke through the downfall to sheen on the road ahead of him and that's when he saw her in his peripheral vision. Kristin McKaslin in her chic tan coat and designer clothes, sitting with her head in her hands, alone behind the long wall of windows.

She was stranded, too. And all by herself. That just wasn't right. He eased the vehicle to the curb with a bump. No way was he going to let her sit there. Not when Providence had handed him a four-wheel drive and, like it or not, he was still heading home.

Through the glass, backlit by fluorescent light, he could see her perfectly, with that short golden bob of her hair falling forward as she sat. He could feel her misery.

Yet although she looked every bit the stranded traveler, Kristin McKaslin was still the picture of perfection in her upscale clothes and her every-hair-in-place do.

It must be nice to have a life like hers. He tried not to hold it against her, and the old envy surprised him. It wasn't exactly envy, but it was close. As a boy growing up, he'd gotten an eyeful of the McKaslins' storybook life via his mom. He saw the Thomas Kinkade-like coziness of the house she'd grown up in, heard endlessly from Mom how the McKaslin girls never gave their mother any grief the way he did. As a kid, his own inadequacies hurt and he was ashamed of them, so he did his best to cover them up with bravado and stupid recklessness.

He'd grown up, tried hard to be a good man. But some things didn't change—like the truth in a man's heart. He'd wanted *that* life. To live in a warm and roomy house with a whole family, instead of in a cramped, tumbling down house with a widowed mom who worked three jobs to keep food on the table. He'd never been able to come to terms with his father's death. Or the simple fact that Mom's life would have been without hardship and he would have grown up differently if his dad had been there.

Maybe—just maybe—his heart would be whole if tragedy hadn't struck.

Let the past go, man. Sometimes it was the only thing he could do. Instead of reexamining a past he couldn't fix, it was better just to do the best he could now, in the moment. And that meant helping Kristin.

The way he figured it, anyone who looked so broken over the thought of missing her family, didn't deserve to be stranded and alone on Thanksgiving. Maybe that was another reason the Lord had made sure a vehicle was available. So that he could offer her a ride.

Ryan liked it when the Father gave him a purpose. It was easier to forget his own troubles and to not think about what awaited him in Montana. He'd worked so hard to stay away since he left for college.

He tapped the horn, hoping she could hear over the wind and through the terminal's walls. Her head popped up and her hands fell away to reveal her heart-shaped face twisted with melancholy. No tears, just emotion so raw it made his chest squeeze with pain.

I'll make sure you get home. He watched her squint through the windows and storm, trying to figure out who was honking. She frowned and looked away. All she probably saw was a strange vehicle lurking outside from where she sat. Okay, she couldn't see through the vehicle's tinted windows. He hit the window lever and the tinted glass slid down, bringing in the storm.

He shivered, but being cold was nothing compared to the look of relief on Kristin's face. The sadness faded like night to dawn and an astonished look replaced it. He gestured for her to come join him.

She lifted one eyebrow, as if making sure of his offer.

He waved her over again. Her beaming smile was the prettiest thing he'd seen in some time. She bounded to her feet, slipped her computer-case strap over one slim shoulder and her garment bag over the other. She marched toward him with a buoyant grace that showed how happy she was.

Yeah, it was a good thing he made the wrong turn and wound up in the right place to help her. Icy wind seared like razor blades through his thin Phoenix-bought coat, but he didn't mind. There was something in the way she hurried toward him that warmed him on the inside. Like a lightbulb's steady glow.

It must be nice to have the kind of home she wanted to get to so badly. He fought a twist in his chest as he climbed out into the snowfall—whatever emotion that was, he refused to deal with it. He was a world-class ignorer of emotions.

Kristin slid to a stop on the icy sidewalk and he steadied her with a hand to her elbow.

"Careful there. I don't want to have to splint a broken leg for you."

"Whew. No, but at least you would be handy to have around if I did fall." She found her balance and eased away from his steadying grip. "I can't believe it's really you. How did you happen to be lucky enough to get a rental car?"

"The angels smiled down on me, I guess." He took her bag off her shoulder and stowed it. "You wouldn't happen to want a lift to Montana, would you?"

"What? Are you kidding me? I thought I'd be stuck in that terminal. I couldn't believe my eyes when I saw you waving at me from behind your steering wheel. For a second there, I thought I was dreaming. This is too good to be true."

"I guess it's your lucky day. Want me to take the computer case, too?"

"What?" She swiped the snow out of her face. And what a pretty face she had, all lit up with joy and happiness. One of the golden McKaslin girls, who had grown up to be a fine woman. It was easy to see her good heart and her sincerity. He'd forgotten there were still women like her in the world.

"Oh, the computer." She rolled her eyes before shrugging the strap off her shoulder. "I'm getting ditzy. Well, ditzier than usual. Too many hours without sleep."

"That makes two of us." He stowed the computer safely between the seat and a suitcase, so it wouldn't slide around. "Don't stand there freezing. Get in the car."

Kristin felt the blush flame from her throat to her hairline. Was she really gawking at the big handsome doctor who looked about as fit as an NFL quarterback? Yeah! She ripped her gaze away from him and hopped into the passenger seat. The slam of the door meant she was safely inside away from him and she could gather her wits.

Why was she acting as though she'd never seen him before? He was Ryan. Mom's friend's kid. The one who drove his family car into the ditch when he was eight.

It was hard to see that bothersome kid in the broad-shouldered, competent man who settled behind the steering wheel. He smelled of snow and winter nights and spicy aftershave. Just right.

And why was she noticing? She was a self-avowed, independent single woman. She was too smart to fall in love with any man. Let alone someone who lived half the country away.

Ryan clicked his belt into place. Grim lines carved deep into the corners around his mouth. "Buckle up. It's gonna be a tough drive."

Kristin hadn't realized the windshield was a solid white sheet until the wipers snapped to life and beat the accumulation away. "The snow is really coming down. Do you think we can get very far?"

"I'm gonna try. We may have to overnight it some-where, *if* we can find a vacancy."

"Sounds sensible. We want to get home safe and sound."

"That's the idea." He winked, put the Jeep in gear and eased down the accelerator. The tires slid, dug in and propelled them forward. "I've got a cell phone if you want to call home. Your folks are probably up worrying."

Was that nice or what? Ryan definitely had done a lot of changing. "Thanks, but I tried with mine. I couldn't get through. The storm."

"Ah." He concentrated on navigating through the whiteout conditions.

She didn't say anything more. If she couldn't make out the road in front of him, how could he? But he was somehow, driving with a steady confidence that made her take a closer look at the man Ryan Sanders had grown up to be.

A volunteer in the Peace Corps. A doctor. He was a man of contradictions. He still had that "I'm trouble" grin and the stubble on his jaw made him look rugged and outdoorsy. Mom was always mentioning Mary's son on her weekly calls, but Kristin had dismissed him along with all the other eligible men Mom talked about.

Poor Mom, who was never going to give up hope for another wedding to plan. What was it Mom had said about Ryan? Kristin couldn't remember. She automatically deleted any talk of men and marriage and how Mr. Right would come along one day.

There was no such thing as Mr. Right! How could Mom be in an unhappy marriage and be so blind to the truth?

Maybe it was how she made it through the day. Troubled, Kristin tried to turn her thoughts away from painful things. Stuff she tried not to think about, but going home only made it impossible to ignore. The hole in her family that remained—Allison. The missing face no one mentioned. The place at the table where a chair used to sit. The oldest sister who'd been alive and beautiful, and whom Kristin had loved with all her heart.

The years passed, her parents had slipped into a resigned distant marriage, her sisters had gone on to make homes and marriages of their own, but some things would never be the same. If there was something Allison's death had taught her, it was that nothing lasted. Nothing. Not family, not love, not life.

Ryan broke the silence that had fallen between them.

"Hey, are you hungry? There's a drive-through that's open. It's the only one I've seen so far. If we don't stop, it might be our last chance to eat until daybreak."

"I'm starving. I definitely want to stop."

"Looks like only the drive-through is open." He braked in the parking lot to study the front doors. "Hope you don't mind eating in here."

"I'm not picky."

"Me, either." He slid to the order board, where the whiteout had blocked out half the menu. "I have no idea if you can see to order anything."

"It's no problem. There's one of these near my town house. I know the menu by heart."

"Me, too." Why that surprised him, Ryan didn't know. It made perfect sense she would eat at restaurants. He just didn't picture her as the fast-food kind of girl.

A mumbling teenager who sounded unenthusiastic about his job took their orders. After waiting at the window while the winds kicked up, blowing the snow sideways, they were handed two sacks of piping-hot food. Ryan crept through the blizzard to park safely beneath the glow of a streetlight.

"Not that any of the light is reaching us," Kristin commented with a wink as she unpacked the first bag.

Ryan flicked on the overhead lamp. "It's weird. I haven't *seen* snow since I went skiing winter vacation of my senior year in college. And it was on the slopes, not falling."

"I bet it never snows in Phoenix."

"Once, but it was just a skiff. The entire city shut down. It was incredible. Had that same amount fallen back home, no one would have blinked twice. I've sure missed real winters."

Wind buffeted the driver's side of the vehicle, and the gust of snow cloaked them entirely from the nighttime world. Kristin shivered with excitement. She loved a good winter storm. "It looks like you're getting your wish. A full-fledged blizzard in the making!"

"Yeah, I'm one lucky guy."

His crooked grin could devastate a less stalwart woman. Kristin gave thanks that she was a dedicated and sworn single gal who had full immunity to a man's hundred-watt charisma. Because if she wasn't, she'd be caught hook, line and sinker.

He probably charmed all the women in the Southwest with that grin, she thought as she clasped her hands together in prayer. She didn't dare glance in Ryan's direction to see if he'd bowed his head. She had grace to say, and she was going to say it.

But Ryan's melted-chocolate baritone broke in before she could begin. "Dear Father, thank you for watching over us. For bringing us together on this night when we had hoped to be with family but found ourselves alone. Please watch over us on our journey north. In your name."

"Amen," they said together.

The whir of the heater and the fury of the storm filled the silence between them. Kristin unclasped her hands and didn't dare to look at the man beside her.

Paper crackled as Ryan dug through the closest sack. The crisp scent of hot greasy Tater Tots filled the air. The overhead dome lamp spotlighted the center console where Ryan was popping the tops off the little plastic salsa containers.

Why was her heart beating as if she'd just finished a ten-kilometer run? Kristin grabbed a straw, ripped off the paper wrapping, stabbed it into her soda and sipped hard. She'd never seen this side of Ryan Sanders before. She could remember him at church through their growing-up years, slumped on the pew next to his mother, staring off into space with the supremely bored look he'd perfected.

That boy had turned into a sincere man of faith? She never would have guessed the troublesome boy she remembered would have become so serious. Where had the real Ryan gone? Not that there was anything wrong with the man he'd turned out to be—not on the surface, anyway.

But what about deep inside? The parts of a person that were harder to discover? That was the real question. And it was why Kristin refused to date. Why she would never marry anyone.

Because you never knew what a person was really like, until it was too late.

"I think this is yours. Extra sour cream." He held out the wrapped taco in his big, capable hands.

Healing hands, Kristin realized, and they looked it. Powerful but circumspect. "Th-thanks."

The food was piping hot, but she hardly noticed as

she unwrapped the chicken taco. Ryan was consuming his beef taco with great gusto. He stopped to nudge the container of hot sauce her way.

"No, too much for me."

"I say, the hotter the better. I can have all of this?"

"Go for it."

"Awesome." He dumped an extreme amount of blistering sauce on his giant soft-shell taco and gave a moan of satisfaction after he took a bite and chewed. "Not nearly hot enough. I like melt-the-lid-off-the-jar hot."

"*There's* the Ryan I remember."

"Hey, I grew up. But I really haven't changed all that much. Down deep. I'm still a country boy at heart."

A country boy? There was nothing obviously country in the polished, well-dressed man seated beside her. He looked as if he'd walked straight off the pages of a magazine. "You've been away from home for what, more than a dozen years?"

"Thirteen, nearly fourteen. What I can't picture is you living in a big city. Why didn't you marry your high-school sweetheart and buy a house near your folks?"

"Because I didn't have a high-school sweetheart." His innocent question took her back to places best left forgotten.

"Why not?"

His question was an innocent one—he didn't know what he was doing to her by asking. The steel around her heart snapped tight into place, blocking out all the painful memories of that time in her life. When her older beloved sister had left home packed for a church retreat and bubbling with excitement, never to return again.

Kristin's entire world changed that day. Nothing had ever been the same.

But Ryan had left the valley for greater things by then. With a football scholarship in hand and a free ride to an out-of-state university, he'd probably only heard about the small-plane crash that had taken several lives at the time. His mom had probably mentioned it to him on the phone when it happened, but it had only been a newsworthy item to him.

That day years ago had tipped her world on its side and showed her the truth. You could surround yourself with family and friends, make a marriage, a home and a family, go to church and pray faithfully, but it couldn't protect a person. Not even God seemed to be able to do that.

The truth was too personal. She'd tried to talk about it before, but no one seemed to understand. Pastor Bill from her hometown church had been wonderful and understanding, but his well-meant advice had been useless. Why did God want to take Allison from them? She'd been beloved by everyone who knew her, and as an older sister, she'd been awesome. She was beautiful and kind, generous and selfless and smart. Anytime Kristin had needed her, her oldest sister had been there, no questions asked.

It wasn't only her sister that she'd lost that day. She'd

seen the world for what it truly was, and she couldn't surround herself with people and things and pretend that if she was faithful enough, nothing could hurt her or those she loved.

Loss was inevitable. It was a part of life she didn't care for, thank you very much. Kristin grabbed a Tater Tot and bit into the crispy, greasy goodness. Ryan was still waiting for an answer as he watched her, unwrapping his third taco.

"I'm just not into the whole marriage and kids thing." She shrugged. It was a cop-out, she knew it, but there was no way this handsome man who probably had left a string of hopeful women pining away in Phoenix would understand.

"You're a career woman. I get it." Ryan chomped into his taco and chewed while he studied her thoughtfully, as if he were assessing her. Seeing something new in her. "Being a doc is great. I love what I do. It's real satisfaction, gives your life meaning, when you love your work."

"Yeah. That's me. I love my job." She did. So, why did her chest feel hollow as she took another bite of her chicken taco?

"I bet you're good at what you do. I can see it." He grabbed two Tater Tots and dragged them through the hot salsa. "You're organized, smart, likable. Efficient, I bet."

"Yeah, and a devoted workaholic."

"Me, too. That's the reason why I'm headed home to Montana after about a billion years of staying away."

"Because you're a workaholic?"

"Yeah. I've always had to stay wherever I was living. First it was because I was in college and I'd stay to get extra hours at whatever part-time job I had. I needed the money, and Mom understood that. But then it was med school and I needed to study. I was an intern and then a resident and there was no way I could get time off. I worked holidays."

"And now you're a doctor with your own practice. You make your own hours, right?"

"I wish." He rolled his eyes. "I'm in control of my schedule more than I have been. But I'm low man on the totem pole. I'm in a practice with some of the top orthopedic surgeons in the Southwest, and they pull rank. Plus, it's that student-loan thing again."

"The one the size of a house?"

"Exactly. Sometimes on Saturdays when I've got paperwork piled as high as my computer monitor, I get this urge to run off and windsurf the day away on Lake Powell."

"You windsurf?"

"I used to. Then I did something really inane. I decided to get engaged."

"You're getting married?"

"I'm not the type, I know. It took me about three months to figure that out after being dragged to a wedding planner to see about seven thousand different kinds of napkins we could get monogrammed, and my life flashed before my eyes. A life with no windsurfing. It didn't work out." He shrugged, as if it didn't bother him a bit. "It was for the best."

Kristin didn't miss the shadows in his eyes. His tone might be light, but there was pain there. She could feel it as tangibly as the cold seeping in from outside. Whatever happened had been complicated and deeply painful.

She tried to think of something comforting to say, but drew a blank. No simple words of comfort or empathy could begin to ease the hurt from wounds in a person's heart. She knew.

"Well, we better get a move on." Ryan cleared his throat as if dismissing his loss or wiping away his sorrow. He crinkled up the paper wrappers, and the sound was as jarring and abrupt as his movements.

Kristin took the last bite of her taco as Ryan switched on the wipers. A few swipes of the blades and the accumulated snow was gone. The twin beams of the headlights reflected back to them in the whiteout conditions.

"Don't worry. I'll keep us safe." He tossed her a roguishly charming wink, before putting the Jeep into gear.

"I wasn't worried." Kristin balled up the wrapper, pretending to be busy and unaffected by the man beside her.

He's unhappy, she realized. Lonely. She knew what that was like. It was like the storm blocking out the glow from the town's lights until there was only the cold darkness and the howl of the worsening storm. As if there could be no light to warm the long drive ahead.

Chapter Three

Ryan swore it felt as if they'd been driving for an eternity, but when he glanced at the clock in the dash, the green numbers showed less than two hours had passed. For one hundred and twenty long minutes they'd been creeping in a vast darkness, closed off from the world, the tenacious storm allowing him to see only a few feet in front of him.

Twice, he'd spotted the faint sudden pinpoint of oncoming headlights. Each vehicle had been traveling as slowly as he was, fighting to stay on the road. He hadn't seen another driver in the past fifty-three minutes in front of him, behind him or on the other side of the double yellow.

Exhaustion made every nerve ending burn. Three times they'd stopped in the small towns off the highway to look for vacancies. No luck. Every other traveler had the same idea. They had no other option than to keep driving.

"How are you doing?" Kristin's soothing alto broke

the long silence between them. "Want to trade off driving?"

"Maybe. I figured we'd switch once we got to the next town."

"Sounds good. If we don't lose track of the road."

"Pray this storm doesn't get any worse." Grim, Ryan recalled all the cases he'd read about in med school where innocent drivers had gotten caught in harsh winter storms and gone off the road. He saw how easily that could happen.

The blizzard closed in with a vengeance. The falling snow began to spin, washing over the windshield with a dizzying speed. The twin beams of the headlights glared on the downpour, reflecting back at him until he lost complete sight of the highway.

"Thank God for the tracks." Kristin leaned forward, straining against her shoulder harness as if to help him watch for signs of danger. As if they were about to plunge off the road and down a ravine.

"Just what I was thinking." Some brave soul was ahead of them. The lone set of tire tracks was rapidly filling with snow, but it was enough to keep him headed in the right direction. His vision blurred and he blinked hard.

Just stay alert, man. He fidgeted in his seat, fighting the belt. He could use the rest of his soda, both the sugar and caffeine would help, but he didn't want to take his hand off the wheel or his attention from the road. There was no way he was going to let anything happen. He had Kristin to keep safe. Mom was waiting for him.

Thank you, Lord, for the help. The tire tracks in the snow unspooled ahead of them like a sign from above guiding them toward home.

Home. If his head wasn't pounding from exhaustion and the effort of concentrating so hard, he could try to get his mind in the right place. He didn't want Mom to see him like this, undecided and unhappy to be walking straight back to his past.

Luckily, driving took all his energy. He didn't have to think about anything other than this moment and keeping the car on the road. It was like driving in a dark tunnel. He glued his attention to the tire tracks barely visible in the sheen of the headlights.

The road beneath them seemed to heave, tossing the SUV around. Fear hit him and he swung the wheel left, but it was too late. A tree bough swiped across the roof. The passenger-side tires dipped low into the pitch of the shoulder.

He saw it all in a flash, the sharp drop, the void of a forest. Already he was picturing what it would be like to crash through those thick limbs and plunge into the darkness, out of control. Flashes of car-accident victims he'd treated in the E.R. haunted him and he fought to stop the inevitable as the top-heavy SUV began to tip.

Please, Lord, he prayed as, teeth gritted, he fought the jolting steering wheel. *A little help, please.* Crashing into old-growth trees was going to be a very bad thing. Time slowed down. He saw the minute detail of the pine needles on the limb swinging toward them. Beside him Kristin gasped, grabbed the dash, expecting the worst, too.

Then, miraculously, the tires dug in. The vehicle swung left toward the level road, and he eased it to a shaking stop. *Thank you, Father.*

Adrenaline pumping, he tried not to think of everything that could have happened, how hurt they could have been and what those tire tracks meant. "That was a close one. Are you okay?"

Sheet white, Kristin studied him with wide eyes. She nodded. "But whoever is in that car isn't."

He didn't answer. He flicked on the overhead dome light to see as he searched the dash for the hazard lights and hit them on. "Check around and see if there's a first-aid kit. Then button up and come with me."

Gone was the hint of the boy he'd been. He was all man, mature and focused. Reaching beneath the seat, Kristin's fingers tapped over the nubby carpet and bumped into a plastic edge. She got down on all fours to extricate the small box and realized that Ryan was already climbing outside. The brutal subzero winds cut through the warm passenger compartment as he slammed the door shut. The night and storm stole him from her sight.

The box came loose. It *was* a first-aid kit, as she'd hoped it would be. Relieved, Kristin twisted back onto the seat, dug her mittens out of her coat. Her door swung open. Ryan stood just outside the light, shadow and substance as she held up the kit for him to see.

He took it from her. "Do you know how close we are to the next town?"

"I'm guessing maybe twelve, thirteen miles." Kristin sank to midcalf in drifting snow. "It might be quicker heading back. We went, what, ten miles?"

It all added up to potential disaster. He ignored the bitter wind and the sting of flakes needling his face. All that mattered was helping the people in that car.

If he could. If it wasn't too late.

He yanked his cell out of his pocket. *Lord, please let this thing work out here.* He hit auto dial and prayed for a signal.

There were no other sounds but the rapid-fire beat of his heart, the tap, tap, tap of snow and the howl of the wind through the trees. He shook his phone, not that it would do a lick of good. *C'mon. Connect.*

He heard the squeak of leather shoes in the compact snow behind him. One glance told him Kristin was managing. He kept in front of her, taking the brunt of the blizzard hiking along the tire tracks as they rolled through a jagged hole in the guardrail and into the darkness.

His phone beeped. He froze in place. He had a signal! There was a ring, and an emergency operator answered. It sounded like a small county station; he could hear the buzz of activity in the background. It was a busy night for the sheriff's department, and about to get busier.

"I have a single-car accident on highway 84." He squinted at the milepost marker hanging from a jagged arm of the guard post and reported the number to the operator.

What was he going to find? His guts twisted as he

swept the miniflashlight on his key ring through the darkness. Nothing. Only horizontal snow in a black void.

Please, Lord, be with whoever is in that vehicle. Or was. Ryan steeled his spine. Prepared for what he might find, he took a step and skidded down a nearly vertical slope.

Not a good sign, either. He dug his heels in before he crashed into a tree. With pine needles cold against his face, he flashed the small light through the underbrush. Nothing. No, wait. There was a faint something. Squinting, Ryan swept the area again. Sure enough, there it was. The edge of a broken taillight reflecting some of the light back at him despite the heavy downpour and thick foliage.

It was enough of a miracle on this brutal night, that Ryan gave thanks as he crashed through limbs and over dormant blackberry bushes, following the ragged trail of tracks that led to a small sedan. The vehicle was dark and still. A very bad sign.

Help me, Father, he prayed as he snapped limbs and tore branches out of his way, sidling along the quiet car.

Too quiet. That couldn't be good. Between shock, trauma and the freezing cold, he didn't expect to find anyone alive.

"Hello?" Calm, focused, he broke the icy layer of snow off the driver's window with the side of his hand. The glow of his flashlight showed a lone driver with a mass of dark curls slumped behind the wheel.

He tried the door and the handle gave. The passenger compartment was cool, but not yet cold. He began talking, calm and steady, in case the young woman could hear him. So she wouldn't be afraid.

He wasn't aware of Kristin crowding close to see if she could help or the snow slicing between his neck and his coat collar or the wind as he worked.

Wow, he's sure something. Kristin's heart hitched as she watched him work, methodical and skilled. He pressed two fingers to the woman's jugular and some of the tension in his shoulders eased. She was alive.

Kristin leaned against the car. She'd never felt so helpless in her life. If a rental car had been available, then she may well have been here alone to help the injured driver. What good could she have done? Ryan was a blessing. He checked the young woman's pupils while talking to her, low and soothing.

I bet he's a great doctor. Admiration for him filled her up. She loved medical dramas on television, but this was something greater. This was real. Somber lines dug deep in Ryan's face as he turned to her in the faint glow from his flashlight. How badly was the woman hurt?

"What can I do to help?"

"Go through the trunk. I'll pull the latch. See if there's anything to wrap her in. Blankets. Sheets. Something. We've got to get her warm."

At least she was alive. That was something. Praying, Kristin scrambled to the back of the car, lifting the trunk after it popped up. How could he be calm and steady? Okay, he was a doctor, he was used to this, but she wasn't. Fear jittered through her veins, leaving her quaking and her fingers clumsy as she began to push through the crowded trunk. Full laundry bags, textbooks, a laptop case… She spied a flashlight and tested it; it worked. She tucked that under her arm.

As she kept digging, Ryan's voice pulled at her like a fish on a line. She was hooked and unable to turn away. Had she ever heard a man sound like that? A deep gravelly baritone that was both hard-edged man and infinitely caring. Powerful and dependable. A man who could make anything right.

Please, Father, help guide his hands tonight. Kristin moved aside a University of Idaho book bag, realizing the young driver was a college student, probably heading home for Thanksgiving, too. Would she be all right?

She wasn't moving. She was unconscious. At least Ryan was here. He knew what to do. Clutching the stadium blanket she'd found beneath the book bag, Kristin carefully picked her way through the knee-deep snow.

Ryan must have heard her coming. Crouched in the open door, he twisted toward her. Worry lines furrowed deep in his forehead, but he managed a strained nod as his gaze pinned on the folded blanket. "Good. That will do just fine."

"How is she?"

"She's trying to stay awake for me." Solemn, he took the blanket in exchange for his cell phone. "I've got dispatch to make this a priority."

Kristin didn't need to ask. She could see the truth in

his eyes. The young college girl could be seriously injured. "What do you need me to do?"

"The car is stable. I'm not worried about it rolling
any farther down the ravine. The trees here are pretty
sturdy. How do you feel about climbing in the back
seat?"

"Sure." Kristin slipped the cell into her coat pocket,
struggling with the stubborn door. Ice cracked around
the handle and she slipped into the rapidly cooling interior of the compact sedan.

The beam of the flashlight danced eerily around the
silent passenger compartment, as Ryan wedged it into
place on the dashboard. The golden stream illuminated
a beaded cross hanging from the rearview mirror, a
small stuffed puppy tucked into the middle console
next to an insulated coffee cup with the name *Samantha* and the Greek symbols of a sorority printed on it.
And then she saw the college girl's thick and beautiful
brown wavy hair matted with blood.

Kristin shivered all the way to her bone marrow. The
only time she'd seen anyone seriously hurt was after the
private plane went down, when Allison had died. Her
sister Kirby had also been in the plane, but had survived.

Kristin had been a freshman in high school, and with
all the time that had passed since, it felt so long ago. But
the images returned as crisp and clear as if they'd happened an hour ago. The fear for her critically injured sister, the beep of machines, the frightening reality of death
as they all waited for Kirby to regain consciousness, ter-

rified that she'd slip away into an irreversible coma and death.

Kirby had survived.

Please, Lord, help this young woman. She was too young to die.

"I need your help," Ryan said, fracturing her thoughts, working quickly as he dug through the first-aid kit with one free hand. "Hold her head and neck steady from behind while I try to stop this bleeding."

"Steady, huh?" That's the last thing she was. Kristin stared at her quivering hands. She took a deep breath. Willed the fear to stop.

"Like this." He guided her hands. "Cradle her as still as you can. She could have a neck injury, and this will minimize any further damage while I work. All right?"

Kristin knew he meant how important this was. The difference between paralysis and movement, between life and death. Her hands had to be rock steady. She made sure of it.

Ryan was unbreakable steel. Checking vitals, applying pressure and bandages, assessing for further injuries. As he worked, he talked low and reassuring.

"Can you hear me, Samantha? I'm a doctor, if you can believe that. And that's Kristin, in the seat behind you. Say hi, Kristin."

"Hi, Samantha."

The injured woman murmured, but nothing more. Kristin felt the slightest of movements beneath her fingertips, the drum of a very slow pulse and the flex of muscles, as if the girl was trying to awaken.

"Hold her steady." Ryan's grave gaze said everything.

Samantha was seriously injured. Without mercy, the storm raged, the snow pounding like rain. Could help even make it through the blizzard in time? There was so little Ryan could do here, with few supplies. She didn't dare say the words aloud. She'd never felt so helpless.

But Ryan looked confident. In charge. He was amazing. Hope seeped into Kristin's heart as she watched his skilled hands working to stanch the flow of blood from several gashes along the girl's hairline. Blood seemed to be everywhere, but he worked on, composed and sure. She saw on his face the dedication she expected a doctor to have. The seriousness.

And something more rare. Compassion.

When he was done, he seemed to give a sigh of relief. He checked his patient's pulse using his wristwatch, frowned and asked for his cell. Shivering and seeming to be unaware of it, he made another call to the county dispatch.

"They're almost here." Ryan handed her the flashlight. "Or so the operator says. It's hard going for them, and with this poor visibility, they could drive right past the Jeep and miss us. Would you mind going up to flag them down?"

"Sure."

His fingers moved into place between hers, supporting Samantha's head and neck with extreme care. She read the fear he held for the young college woman in his shadowed eyes. She remembered when her sister Kirby had been in intensive care. She knew exactly what hung in the balance. A life. She knew all that meant, truly meant, unlike so many people who went around living lives they took for granted.

All it took was a split second for everything to change. For life to never be the same again. Would Samantha live? Would she be in a wheelchair or on crutches for the years to come?

Holding on to hope for the best outcome, Kristin scrambled up the slope, fighting the wind and snow driving at her back and the brambles grabbing at her feet. The shadows she saw in Ryan's eyes stayed with her as she fought to the top. Shadows of grief that broke her heart as she burst onto the lonely expanse of country road, where no other soul stirred on this cruel night. And so she waited, shivering and alone, for help that felt as if it would never come.

The rumble of the fire truck's engines, muffled by the snow, faded into the distance. Although the taillights had long faded, Kristin watched. She couldn't get the injured college student out of her mind.

Ryan marched toward her, swiping snow out of his eyes as he crossed in front of the SUV's headlights. Burnished by light, surrounded by darkness, he looked more myth than man as he yanked open the passenger door for her.

Woodenly she eased into the seat, stiff with cold, but not feeling anything but a horrible void. Tepid air breezed out of the vents in the dash and she couldn't feel it. The clock glowed the time—not thirty minutes had passed since they'd nearly followed Samantha Fields off the road.

Snow drifted inside with Ryan as he collapsed in the seat and slammed the door. He filled the seat, slumping with his head rolling back against the headrest. His presence made the passenger compartment shrink. "I was able to get through to Tim, a friend I used to work with. He's one of the best surgeons in this area, and he's agreed to meet Samantha at the hospital. He'll take excellent care of her."

"You took the time to do that?"

"Sure. Helping people is what I do. It's why I studied all those years. Why I'm in debt for a few hundred grand." Although exhaustion lined his face and bruised the skin beneath his eyes, his wink was saucy.

She had watched while he worked tirelessly alongside the medics stabilizing Samantha's neck and spine so that she had the best possible outcome, in case of a spinal cord injury. All in a day's work for him, maybe, but she'd never seen anyone like him.

She pulled off her mittens, now that the heater was kicking out a decent hot breeze. "Let's trade places. I'll drive and let you sit here and warm your hands. You've got to be half frozen."

"The cold never used to bother me. I've been away from Montana too long. It's the Phoenix weather. It's thinned my blood. Now I turn into an icicle the second it snows. It's not manly. It's embarrassing."

"I'm embarrassed for you." She'd never met a better example of what a man should be, but he seemed unaware that he was that and more. "Move. Go on. I can't drive from over here."

As if too exhausted to lift his head from the seat back, Ryan swiveled his eyes to focus on her with a disbelieving look. One eyebrow crooked with obvious skepticism. "You'd really drive? You're not just saying that, right?"

"Right."

"You're not afraid to drive in this stuff?"

"Do I look as if I'm shaking in my boots? No."

"But you're a *girl. Girls* don't drive in lots of snow. At least not in my experience."

"You *have* lived in Arizona too long!" Kristin took one look at the man slouching beside her, dappled with big flakes of melting snow, his face chapped from the bitter temperatures outside. "Don't let the designer clothes fool you. You can take the girl out of Montana, but not Montana out of the girl. Let me behind the wheel and I'll show you."

"Yeah? I'd be grateful if I could just close my eyes for about ten minutes."

"How about all the way until the next town?"

"Deal." Ryan opened the door and shouldered out into the dark. "No, you climb over and stay inside. I'll brave the storm. I'm still frozen anyway."

With a lopsided grin, he was gone, leaving the scent of wind, a hint of expensive cologne and man. A pleasant combination. Kristin climbed over the console and into the seat that was pushed too far back for her feet to reach the pedals. She adjusted the seat, snapped the shoulder harness into place and checked out the controls.

Ryan cut through the headlights with that confident, jaunty walk of his. He was like a hero out of an old black-and-white movie, tough and strong and compassionate. She didn't know they made men like that anymore.

He collapsed beside her, bringing with him the frigid wind and a blast of snow. He swiped icy flakes off his eyebrows. "Believe it or not, the blizzard's winding down some."

"Some. Not a lot." Kristin switched off the hazard lights, staring into the impenetrable conditions. No cars had passed, except for the emergency vehicles, since they'd arrived. The road ahead lay like a pristine ribbon of white rolling out of the reach of the headlights. Dangerous driving ahead. Kristin released the hand brake and shifted into low gear.

Ryan unzipped his coat, settling in. "Just tell me if you get too white-knuckled."

"Don't worry. I can handle it. Belt up and hold on." Was he a skeptic or what? It had been a long time since she'd driven anything with more power than her sensible sedan, but she was used to this weather. She hadn't always flown home. She'd driven more often than not over the treacherous mountain passes and she was still in one piece. "This is nothing compared to commuting in Seattle traffic twice a day for more years than I care to count."

"That's what I can't picture. You living in a city. I don't know why. It just doesn't go with the McKaslin image."

"I won't say it wasn't a big adjustment when I first moved there. When I went to college, I thought Bozeman was a big city."

"Bozeman?" he asked.

"Yeah, I know. It's a tiny city compared to someplace like Seattle. I felt lost. Every time I left my apartment I got turned around. I'd never seen so many streets and roads and freeways in my life."

"I know how you felt—moving away from a place with one main street through town, where you know all the roads and shortcuts by heart, to a huge city where the checkers at the grocery store ask for ID because they don't know you, your family, your grandparents and all your cousins by name."

"See, that's where we differ. I didn't mind living someplace folks didn't know me."

Ryan leaned the seat all the way back and stretched out his legs as far as he could. Not comfortable, but an acceptable snoozing position. Except thinking about his past made him antsy. As tired as he was, his nerve endings felt as though they were twitching and his muscles felt heavy as lead. His emotions were going every which way. Regret, guilt, grief.

Nothing Kristin would understand. Some people, like her, could go home again. They would always know the warmth of their childhood awaited them, that the ghosts of memories from holidays past were happy ones. Not haunted by what should have been, and more failures than the young boy he'd been could cope with.

Or the man he'd become.

He liked to think he wasn't a coward. He faced challenges head-on. Sucked it up and did what needed to be done. He wasn't afraid of hardship or hard work. But some things were best left unexamined. Some memories best left buried. He had a good life, he made a good living, and he loved his work and his practice. What good was having to pick apart a past that only brought pain? That exposed wounds that could never be healed?

No, Kristin didn't look as though she'd rather be running away instead of heading home. Her delicate profile was brushed by the glow of the dash lights, burnishing her creamy porcelain-fine skin, the feminine line of her nose and the dainty cut of her chin. He supposed her parents would welcome her with open arms, and tomorrow there would be only happiness in her home where her sisters and their families gathered to make new memories for the holidays to come.

He closed his eyes, wondering, just wondering. If he would have turned out the same if his dad had lived instead of withered away in a coma. If the logging truck hadn't crossed the double yellow on the road to town. If, instead of being struck and pinned to the ground beneath a load of logs, Dad had returned home with the ice cream he'd gone to fetch.

God made all things for a reason. But what about tonight? Why had Samantha Fields been hurt tonight? How would her life be changed?

Only God knew.

Still, it troubled him deeply. He closed his eyes, too troubled to fall right asleep. Listening to the swipe of the wiper blades on the windshield, he felt the blast of heat from the vents. The vehicle fishtailed now and then, and Kristin handled it skillfully, keeping them safe as they journeyed through the dark and snow. He couldn't remember feeling more lonely as the hours dragged on and sleep claimed him, blessedly deep.

Chapter Four

Something was hurting his eyes. Something shiny. Bright like sunlight.

Consciousness returned in a nanosecond—the ache in his back from the seat, the binding restriction of the seat belt, the hum of the engine and low murmur of music on the radio. And Kristin, with her golden hair tangled and windblown, and fatigue bruising the fragile skin beneath her eyes. She smiled, and he swore he could see heaven.

"Good morning." Her gentle alto was the single most beautiful sound he'd ever heard. A *good* way to start a new day. Thanksgiving Day.

Rational thought pierced through his sleep-fogged mind. Kristin had let him sleep through until daybreak. Sitting upright, he swiped a hand over his face and looked around. Sure enough there was that celebratory shine of the rising sun cresting the granite peaks to the east.

Even though he hadn't seen those particular mountains in more than a decade, he recognized the rugged snow-blanketed peaks thrusting into the silky wisps of clouds and sun.

The Bridger Range. Mountains he'd climbed in, biked in, hiked in and skied on. Where he would take off just to get away. Where he retreated just to play. Every morning he'd sat at the breakfast table shoveling in bowl after bowl of cereal while he stared through the old warped glass windows and there they were, those mountains jagged and snowcapped and close enough to touch.

Mountains he hadn't seen since he was a restless eighteen-year-old who couldn't wait to leave the prison of his small town. Who'd never looked over his shoulder as he drove away.

Looking at those proud summits and those breathtaking slopes made it real. He was home. For better or worse. "I only meant to catch a few z's. Not sleep through three mountain passes and two states. You should have kicked me in the shin to wake me up."

"It was tempting, but I didn't mind driving. It was the least I could do, considering you were so valiant saving Samantha's life."

"Valiant? Me? No way. I just tried to get her stable. That reminds me, I meant to check on her before this." He dug around in his pockets for his cell, but he only got Tim's voice mail. He left a message, there was nothing else he could do for now. "What about you? You drove through a blizzard for hours."

"They had just plowed, so it wasn't too bad."

"You had to stop for gas. Why didn't you wake me up so I could take the next shift?"

"Oh, I tried. I shook you and you didn't even move. You were so out of it you slept right through the ding when I left the keys in the ignition and the banging when I filled the tank. A truck at the next fuel pump accidentally hit his horn and nothing. Not even the slightest hitch in your snoring."

"I don't snore."

"That you know."

He didn't snore, but Kristin couldn't resist teasing him. He looked adorable, all rumpled and sleep-soft. He'd sprawled all over his side of the vehicle, and he drew his legs up and yawned widely.

As much as she was *so* not interested romantically, the woman in her couldn't help appreciating a fine, good-hearted man. If she wasn't careful, she'd be crazy enough to start developing a crush on him. He was a doctor, he made a difference with his life, he was handsome and kind and funny and smart.

He's probably commitment shy and has a list of typical male faults a mile long, she thought to intentionally counterbalance the admiration glowing in her chest like the rising sun.

He rubbed his eyes and his nose. Scrunching up his mouth like a little kid, he looked ten times more handsome as he did. He blinked, as if his eyes were still trying to focus on the rolling mountain valley and the dazzling peaks rimming it. "Look, the snow's stopped."

"Yeah. About an hour ago. There's nothing like a

Montana morning." Her eyes hurt with the beauty of it. She was home. Rose-hued sunlight shimmered on miles of quiet, pristine snow, like thousands of tiny faceted jewels flung across the land. A land so big and untamed, it still felt wild over a century after it was settled.

Wooden fence posts draped in snow marched along meadows and over undulating hills, not unlike the fences the pioneers had sunk into this land. Up ahead an elk, a light milk-chocolate tan against the dazzling snow, ambled onto the two-lane highway. He swiveled his elegant head to look at her, his polished antlers gleaming like ivory in the light.

She slowed on the recently plowed roadway. Ice had her fishtailing but she steered into it, shifted into neutral and eased to a stop. With no traffic so early in this desolate place, she waited instead of going around.

"I haven't seen that in a while." Ryan breathed, sitting up straight. "We used to have a whole herd of them that would graze in the fields next to our house."

"We did, too. They'd come and eat the grain set out for the horses."

"Is he awesome or what?"

Pure, elegant power, the male elk lifted his head to scent the wind. Muscles rippled beneath his tan coat as he stretched. As if sensing danger, the great animal gathered up into a breathtaking leap. Agile and lithe, the bull galloped across the ruby-hued landscape, a streak of brown against the wonder of the dawn. A ray of sunlight haloed him and he vanished.

"Awesome," Kristin agreed into the silence.

As the SUV crept forward on the ribbon of road, Ryan fought the memories crowding up from the deep well in his heart he'd boarded shut decades ago. Memories of the crisp winter air searing his face. His boots sinking deep in the snow as he tried to walk in his dad's tracks, though the footprints were too far apart. The crackle of the dried marsh reeds as they rustled when Dad knelt down. The black stock of his hunting rifle resting on his thigh.

"What made these tracks, son?" Dad had asked in that hushed voice he used, not as harsh as a whisper but so quiet Ryan had to scoot up closer to hear. "Look carefully."

His eight-year-old body had been thrumming with excitement. He hitched up the woolen hat that had slung too low and into his eyes, and frowned at the tracks. They looked just like the deer tracks they saw on the north side of the marsh. But he didn't want to blurt out the wrong answer without thinking long and hard on it first. He didn't want to disappoint his dad.

"Here's a hint. First figure about how long they are."

"I shoulda known that right off, Dad!" Ryan remembered to keep his voice down even if he wanted to shout with excitement. "It's an elk. Elks' tracks are bigger than deer. And, uh, it's a bull elk. He'd been polishin' up his antlers on that cottonwood. The bark's all gone in spots."

"That's my smart boy. My guess is if we move along nice and quiet, we just might be lucky enough to get a good look at him."

The rasping hum of a diesel engine tore Ryan from the past and from his father's side. He sat with the morning sun stinging his eyes in the passenger seat as Kristin merged onto the wide-open lanes of I-90. The three-trailer semi barreling along in the lane beside them pulled ahead, the driver in an obvious hurry to get home.

Home. How was he going to make it through the next twenty-four hours when he hadn't even reached his mom's house and he was already dragging up the past? And feeling torn apart by it. He didn't know. He didn't have any answers. He flipped down the visor and winced at his reflection in the mirror. He took one look at his red-rimmed eyes, dark spikes of hair that looked like a twister tore through them and a day's growth shadowing his jaw.

Yeah, Mom's gonna take one look at me and start right in. Ryan could hear it already. She'd want to know if he was sleeping enough, eating right, et cetera, et cetera, and there was no way he could tell her the truth. No way he could drag up the past that would only devastate them both. For her sake, he had to be tough.

Troubled, he stared out his side of the windshield and blinked. It was the marsh. Buried in snow, the surface rough and choppy due to a few of the hardier, taller reeds and cattails poking through the snow. The marsh where Dad would take him to learn what a man needed to know.

It wasn't the hunting. It wasn't the tracking. It was the self-reliance. *The world's a harsh place, son.* He could hear Dad's mellow baritone as clear and true as the day he'd said it. *A smart man adapts and perseveres and learns to take care of himself. Look, there's the elk.*

Ryan saw it perfectly in memory—the proud bull poised at the frozen shore, antlered head lifted to scent the wind on a morning lit by gold and rose, in a world layered with white.

Yeah, Dad, you sure taught me that lesson well. Ryan swallowed past the knot in his throat, turning his head to watch as the marsh whizzed by and fell behind them. Lost from sight like the past. Yeah, his dad's death taught him way too much. He'd learned to take care of himself at an early age.

"This is our exit." Kristin's voice sounded thick.

With excitement? Probably. She had her family waiting, her sisters coming home, her grandparents to draw near. Self-reliance wasn't something a McKaslin girl needed to know to survive. He realized what felt like envy was really longing. Longing for what could never be.

You can't change the past, man, he told himself, although he knew that lesson well, too. The past is gone, done, no sense in letting it in. He was changed. A man he hoped his dad would be proud of. Someone who was about as self-reliant as possible in this world of Internet and cell phones, of urban sprawl and shopping malls.

"Look." Kristin gestured ahead as she circled off the icy ramp and onto the two-lane road that nosed them toward town. "A lot has changed. Oh, that restaurant is new. There's Gramma's coffee shop. She has a new awning out front. I'll have to tell her how cute it looks."

Ryan scanned the green-and-white-striped awning giving a decidedly *Country Living* look to the shop that advertised "Espresso" in loopy purple neon. That was the coffee place Mom was always talking about. She'd picked up extra work whenever Kristin's grandmother needed help.

That's when he realized the town, with its old-fashioned main street and neat, sturdy buildings that hadn't changed since the fifties, had grown up, too. A few quaint restaurants, more cafés than the old red Formica-countered diners, brightened up the faded brick buildings marching down the length of several blocks. Corey's Hardware had a new neon sign, fresh paint and a bench out front.

There was a new antique store prettied up with lace curtains in the wide windows. And the Sunshine Café, where, after he'd saved up change from collecting aluminum, he'd splurge on chocolate milkshakes for him and his little sister before handing over the bulk of the hard-earned dollars to his mom.

"Do your cousins still run that place?"

"Yeah. They make the best chocolate shakes anywhere."

"I was just thinking about that. Thick and sweet and so chocolaty." Ryan's stomach growled. "Wow, I remember you and your sisters would ride your horses into town and tie them up in the parking spots in front of the café."

"And you would ride your bike."

His bike. As Kristin navigated along the snowy street, where previous tracks of chained-up vehicles had broken a clear path, he saw snatches of the boy he'd been. Pedaling on his secondhand mountain bike down the wrong side of the road, a rebel without a cause and a chip on his shoulder. Holding down two jobs, bagging at the grocery on weekends and cleaning barns for Kristin's uncle. Wanting his mother's life to be easier. Hating that it wasn't. Missing his dad so much, it hurt to breathe.

I never should have come back, he thought, his eyes stinging. It was too much. Earlier, he'd vowed to keep his thoughts in the present. But what did a guy do when the past was tangled up with the present?

"The closer we get to home, the sadder you look." Kristin sounded concerned. Caring, the way a friend was.

He lived such a busy life, he didn't have a lot of friends. And he liked it that way. He shrugged. His problems were his own. "I'm just dog tired. You doin' okay? I could take over. In fact, why don't you let me drive?"

"Because those are my dad's fields. Okay, they're my sister's now. Michelle and her husband took over the farming. I'm almost *home*."

Kristin probably didn't realize how much warmth she placed on that word. Her emotion came through as easily as if she'd opened wide her heart. What a blessing she had, in the family she'd grown up with. In the childhood home that rose into sight nestled on the crest of a low rolling hill. The front windows reflected mauve in the rising sun, and the clouds overhead began spitting out tiny airy flakes of snow, as delicate as spun sugar. Like a blessing on this day of homecoming.

"I get to see how my new baby nieces are growing. Now I'm getting excited! The last time I came home, it was when little Caitlin was born."

"I take it Caitlin belongs to one of your sisters?"

"Yep. I'm a proud aunt many times over." Okay, there were a hundred excellent reasons for coming home. Her sisters were married, and when they all gathered together for holidays, they'd become a sizable group. It was exciting to see how happy her sisters were. Happy with the lives they'd chosen. Her sisters were mothers now, and that meant a whole troop of nieces and nephews she got to spoil.

Both bitter and sweet, her visits home. Very hard on her poor heart.

"That's a pleasure I haven't enjoyed yet, being Uncle Ryan." For the first time on the trip, he smiled, genuine and true, and it was as if his defenses lowered and she could see more deeply into him. See a glimpse of his dreams. "Mia has just finished vet school. She's worked hard to get this far, and she hasn't taken the time to fall in love."

"She's smart, finishing her school first." It's what she did. "A woman has to be able to make a living on her own."

"That's what Mia says, and I agreed. Look at my

mom. She married Dad right out of high school. They had a happy marriage until the day he was struck by that truck. It was hard enough facing each day without him there, for all of us, but we struggled financially, too. In a small town with no training whatsoever, Mom cleaned houses and worked at the cannery outside Bozeman. Yet no matter how we all worked, it was never enough to make ends meet. It was hard for her. Mia and me—"

He paused, raked his hand through his dark hair and turned to stare out the window. His throat worked. "We did everything we could to make it easier for her, but it was a hard road to walk."

He fell silent, gazing off into the fields where tender shoots of winter wheat hid beneath the numbing comfort of snow. Like the anguish that Ryan clearly worked so hard to hide. Kristin's heart twisted so hard it hurt to breathe, and she trained her attention where it belonged—on the road and not on a man's silent pain.

She remembered a strong-willed boy who was a little too loud, a tad too reckless. He'd been in the background of her growing-up years, not someone she hung out with. Sure, she'd known he'd lost his dad and that his mom worked a lot. But she'd been a girl herself, and then a teenager too caught up in friends and school and her own family's loss to have given more than a passing thought to a boy who was nothing but trouble.

That boy's pain was in the man, a tangible presence that ached like a festered wound. One that had tried to heal over the years, but could not.

She knew what that was like. Some wounds could

never close. Some hurts always ached. Some tragedies changed a person forever.

She drove in stinging silence until her parents' house rose up on the road before them, graced by the soft morning's glow. The ache inside her eased. The familiar sight of the big wraparound porch, the wide old-fashioned windows, the lights from the kitchen where Mom was already hard at work caused emotion to ball in her throat. She was *home*.

Ryan broke the silence. "It's just like I remember it."

"It's always the same. A safe place to come to." But not an easy place. The tangle of opposing emotions left her feeling conflicted—as always. Mom and Dad's sadness, their strained marriage, Allison's loss that was never spoken of. *Never.*

And the good things, too: the laughter of her sisters over dinner, playing Monopoly after the dishes were done to the sounds of the football game from the living room. Gramma's loving presence. Nephews and nieces to hold close.

She hesitated. A busy day awaited her in the house that loomed over them, casting them in partial shadow. "Will you be all right?"

"Sure." He nodded, but his smile was shallow and didn't light his eyes. He looked faraway, as if his thoughts were troubled and elsewhere. He looked tired as he swiped his palm over his face. "Thanks for driving, Kristin. You didn't have to let me sleep."

"I figured Samantha's savior deserved some rest. If you hear how she's doing, will you let me know?"

"Sure. I should reimburse you for the gas."

"Oh, no. Consider it my contribution. It's the least I can do. If you hadn't come along, then I'd be in Boise right now."

"Look, there's your mom." Ryan saw the woman who'd aged since the last time he saw her long ago. He didn't know why that surprised him, it was completely logical. Time passed and it changed everyone. But to see the woman who used to be so young-looking with gray accenting her golden hair and her face lined from hardship—he felt it down deep.

Everyone had hardship. Life had trials, and it wasn't the bad things that happened but the way a person rose to the challenge that mattered. He had lost a father. Alice McKaslin had lost a daughter. The worry clear on her face turned to relief when she recognized Kristin behind the wheel of the SUV.

"Kristin! There you are! Oh, we were so worried!" Alice, still in her quilted housecoat and matching quilted slippers flew down the snow-covered steps.

"Didn't you get my message?" Kristin asked, hopping into the cold, closing the door behind her as she cut behind the vehicle and out of sight.

In the side-view mirror, Ryan could see Kristin step into her mother's outstretched arms. The love unmistakable on Kristin's face, shining in her eyes, made her glow.

Family. Yeah, it was important, but he wasn't looking forward to the price of it. He loved his mom. He'd do anything for her. But he couldn't look anywhere without seeing the past. Even the fields where he'd worked long and brutal days in hundred-degree heat bringing in hay for Mr. McKaslin brought memories flooding back. He dreaded the drive back to town, where he would see more of the past, more of the boy he'd been. More of the turmoil and pain he'd worked so hard to leave behind.

While mother and daughter were still holding on to each other and exchanging greetings, he climbed out and grabbed her computer case and bag.

"Why, Ryan Sanders, is that you?" Alice McKaslin noticed him trying to slink past.

He'd wanted to avoid the gooey mess of female emotions if he could, but no such luck. So he faced the teary-eyed females with a man's courage. "It's me. It's good to see you, Mrs. McKaslin. Happy Thanksgiving."

"Why, happy Thanksgiving to you! Your mom has been talking of nothing else for weeks. She's baked every last one of your favorite treats, I hope you know."

"I figured she would." He froze, knowing what was next, but he couldn't do anything to stop it. Mrs. McKaslin released her daughter and came at him next, her arms outstretched, to give him a hug. "What on earth are you two doing together?"

"It's a long story. I'm sure you can get Kristin to tell you. I've got to get home. Mom's probably worried about me. I was supposed to come in last night."

"Come here and let me hug you, young man."

"Oh, I wouldn't do that if I were you. I haven't shaved. Showered. Been deloused."

"Oh, you can still make me laugh." Refusing to back

down, Alice came at him and wrapped him into a kindly hug and, being a self-reliant man, he endured it—okay, it was nice. Alice was like a dear aunt to him when he'd been growing up. He brushed her cheek with a brief kiss as he moved out of her embrace.

"You're more handsome up close than in those pictures your mom shows me. You don't see her enough, young man."

Standing behind her mother, Kristin winked at him. "Go easy on him. He's a busy, important doctor and the only reason I'm here and not snowed in at Boise is because he's a good guy."

"You're not so bad yourself, Miss McKaslin." The way both women were looking at him, as if he'd hung the moon and lit the stars, made him itchy.

He was uncomfortable with looks like that. With anyone getting too close. He'd gotten used to being alone. That was why Francine had returned his ring last September. He didn't need her at all, she'd said.

It was time to go. He let Alice lead the way to the front door, ignoring Kristin when she gestured for her bags. He was a lot of things, but he tried to use his manners when he had them. And what Kristin had done for him, in letting him sleep, he appreciated more than she could ever know. She looked as exhausted as he'd felt before getting some shut-eye, and he didn't mind at all carrying her bags into the house and depositing them at the top of the stairs.

"You didn't have to do that." She looked at him as if she appreciated the gesture. "But thank you."

"No problem." The delicious aroma scenting the

house—apple and pumpkin pies, frying bacon and the roasting warmth of a baking turkey made his stomach growl loudly. He blushed. "Sorry about that."

"Would you like to stay? Breakfast is in the works. Eggs and bacon and pancakes and sausage. Real home-made hash browns."

"I can't tell you how good that sounds, but Mom would box my ears. I'd best get home. She's waiting for me, and I'm late. I'm probably in trouble. Wow, I haven't said that since I was eighteen."

"Some things never change." Kristin breezed down the stairs, aware of her embarrassing grade-school pictures marching along the wall at her elbow. Hopefully, he wouldn't notice.

He didn't say anything as he headed for the door. "Take care of yourself, Miss McKaslin."

"You too, Dr. Sanders."

She didn't know why, but she hated seeing him slip through the door and stride down the steps. Even in the slick conditions, he walked with an athlete's assurance. With the power of a man who had confidence and integrity. Inside she sighed a little, remembering how he'd probably saved a young woman's life.

"Kristin, honey, close the door, would you?"

"What?" She shook her head, realizing she was letting in all the cold air. Shivering, she shut the door but watched through the window as Ryan climbed into the rented vehicle, belted in and drove away, leaving her behind. Adding another ache to the others she was collecting inside her heart.

Chapter Five

Ryan took one look at his childhood home and wanted to keep driving right past the unplowed driveway. *I'm not ready for this.*

He was in his thirties. If he wasn't ready now, when would he be? He'd nearly been away from Montana more years than he'd lived here. How could it be that time looped back upon itself so that as he spun the wheel to the right, slipping and sliding on the fresh snow, he saw the past more clearly than the world in front of him?

The small wooden, open-faced shed that sided the road looked every bit the same. His dad had built it to keep him out of the weather while he waited for the bus as a nervous first grader, with his superhero lunchbox in hand.

The hill, grown over with sturdy young trees now, that Dad had cleared and they'd used as a sled run during the long winters. The sounds of younger Mia's delighted screams as she slid down the slope on an inner tube, the low rumble of Dad's laughter and Mom's gentle chiming voice as she brought out a thermos of hot chocolate to keep them warm as they played.

The past haunted him with every turn of the wheels as he slowed to a stop along a private road where a small ranch house with brand-new siding and vinyl windows waited quietly. It wasn't the same house he remembered. Mom had made improvements over the years. She'd had a front porch built. She always admired the McKaslins' and could never afford the lumber for him to build her one when he was growing up.

Snow carpeted it now and clung like vanilla icing to the rails and steps. The large front window was shadowed, but a generous gray plume of smoke rose from the stovepipe. Homey. He grabbed his overnight bag and loped through the snowfall, snapped open the gate that was new and didn't squeak, and went around to the back door.

A glad brightness shone from the new bay windows—he'd sent Mom the money for the kitchen remodel as last year's Christmas present, and now he could see directly into the small kitchen and eating area. There was Mom, dressed in her usual worn jeans and a sweatshirt, her thick hair caught up in dainty clips, a crisp white apron at her waist as she stirred something at the stove.

Once again, the past and the present merged. Like every day of his childhood, she'd made breakfast at the stove while she hummed her favorite inspirational songs and sipped a cup of coffee laced with hazelnut coffee creamer. Only the two years following Dad's death, she hadn't sung once. Not once. Not even in church.

Slowly, over time, the music had returned to her life. But there had never been another man in this house. Until now.

Knowing the door was unlocked, as it had been all his life, he turned the handle so he could see the look on Mom's face as she turned. Her eyes widened and her mouth opened; tears gleamed in the same instant she dropped the spatula on the counter, the eggs forgotten.

"Ryan!" As if he'd just rescued the world from certain disaster, she ran to him. "You're home! You're here. I can't believe it! Oh, it's so *good* to see you!"

Happiness lit his heart as he dropped his bag, opened wide his arms and hugged his mom to his chest. She was a little thing, wrapping her arms around him, smelling of coffee and shampoo and the lilac lotion she'd always used. Her laughter bubbled through him as she stepped back and studied him with a mother's keen, knowing gaze.

"You're going to be the death of me, young man. I was worried out of my mind, what with this weather and your flight diverted. Yes, I checked with the airport. You could have *called* and let me know you were *alive*."

Okay, so no matter how old a man was, his mom was always his mom. "I know. I should have called and I meant to, but stuff happened. Are you gonna ground me?"

"I have half a mind to do it, too!" But her eyes were

laughing and crying at the same time. "Oh, son, you look awful. You're not getting enough sleep. You're working too hard."

"I've just got a lot of stuff going on right now—"

"You stop sending me money, right now. You're not taking care of yourself. Have you eaten?"

"Uh, no. Nothing was exactly open, since we drove up through the middle of nowhere."

"We?"

Boy, did Mom jump on that quick, or what? And how was he going to minimize the fallout? He'd tell her the truth, he wasn't the kind of man to lie to his mother, and then she'd get all excited because he'd spent time with a woman. And not just with any woman, but with her best friend's daughter. Wasn't that just what she'd been hoping for all these years? For him to marry one of the nice McKaslin girls?

Yeah, right. He wasn't the marrying kind. He'd always suspected it, but Francine had been all the proof he needed. The last thing he wanted was to settle down. Not that Mom was going to understand that. Not in the slightest.

Look at the way she was practically vibrating with hope. He knew his mom, and she was secretly praying right now, as she retrieved her spatula and rescued the eggs from the frying pan, that he was going to say he'd driven up from Boise with a woman. A special woman.

And the second he admitted it was Kristin, she'd leap ahead and draw her own conclusions and there was nothing he could do to stop her. It would snowball into this big thing, when the truth was simple. He'd offered her a ride. She'd accepted. That was it. End of story.

"A stranded traveler I picked up at the airport, that's all." He shrugged out of his coat and dropped it on his suitcase. "And before you start getting all crazy, it was one of the McKaslin girls. She was alone and it wasn't safe for her to spend the night in a strange city."

"Oh, I should hope not!" Mom lit up, shining as if she was about to spontaneously emit her own energy field. "Kristin McKaslin. My, my. You know, she's got some fancy job on the coast. Alice was just saying—"

As if on cue, the phone rang. Mom lifted the eggs from the pan with her spatula. He was gentleman enough to hold out the platter for her and carry it to the table as she raced for the phone.

"Oh, Alice! Yes, Ryan told me. Isn't that something? On the same flight from Seattle?"

Yep, some things never changed. Mom was an eternal optimist, and he was an affirmed bachelor. How could he be anything else? There were only three chairs at the table, in the nook that had been widened to accommodate the same wooden table Mom had bought after her wedding long ago. It had been refinished and looked as good as new sitting on the braided rug on the polished hardwood floor. Although the room had changed, life went on.

But the little boy who'd lost what mattered most—his father—and the grown man who watched people die every day in the emergency room in the hospital he was affiliated with had taught him one thing. Nothing in life was guaranteed. The only certain thing was God's grace, that was all, and getting close to people was a fool's quest. It was bound to end. People died, and their love went with them, and that was it.

While his mom chatted with her lifelong best friend, he rescued the bacon and sausage links from the oven and set four slices of bread to toasting. Just as he did when he was a kid. He settled into his chair at the table, facing the windows that looked out over the meadows and forested hills to the giant jagged mountains that were shrouded with clouds.

He couldn't say why his heart felt as if it was shattering all over again, and the pain was blinding. He blinked hard as he gulped down orange juice, the past like a ghost standing behind him, and the future as hard to see through as the clouds at the horizon, bringing more snow.

Over the sounds of Dad and the brothers-in-law settling into the football game, Kristin scooped the newest addition to the family out of the playpen and into her arms. Four-month-old Caitlin with her curls of gold gave a final outcry before settling against Kristin's shoulder with a whimper of relief.

"You just wanted to be held, huh?"

As if in agreement, the infant relaxed in Kristin's arms. So precious. She brushed a hand over Caitlin's soft, soft hair. So fine and downy it was like touching the most heavenly cloud. With the drowsy baby falling back to sleep, Kristin rocked her gently from side to side, beneath the new collection of framed pictures Mom had started on the wall.

Photos of the six grandchildren filled the space between the living room and kitchen, from newborn to christening to every stage along the way. The newest picture of Kirby's son, Michael, dressed up like a fighter pilot for the church's Harvest festival. Karen's two girls, Allie in a ballerina's costume and one-year-old Anna in a bunny suit. Michelle's Emily taking her first steps captured forever with Dad holding out his strong, capable hands for her to toddle to.

It was what was missing that made her eyes burn. If Allison had lived, she would have married, and her children would be on this wall, too. Sadness gathered inside her until she had to turn away.

If Allison had lived, then Kristin's life would have been different, too. Mom and Dad wouldn't have fallen away from one another in their grief. The family would have remained whole. And Kristin would have been different, too.

She closed her eyes and turned away, willing down the memory of taking a calculus test one moment and the next having her safe world torn to shreds as the principal interrupted to pull her out of class. Her dad was waiting in the office to tell her of her sister's death.

"Oh, did you see the latest addition?" Mom appeared around the corner, her full apron smudged with flour from the rolls she'd been making. Wiping her hands on a dish towel, she gestured toward a golden framed photograph. "Caitlin's christening. It was a shame you missed it."

Kristin knew her mom didn't understand. Over half of the company's business rode on their clients' successes at the trade shows. Her boss had refused her request for a day off flat out. "I'm here now. Do you need more help in the kitchen?"

"Don't change the subject, young lady." Mom gave her sternest look, but it faded away as she studied the pictures. "I expect your little one to be on this wall one day. I understand you like having a career, it must be exciting to live in a big city, but your roots are here, Kristin. Your family is here."

It was an old argument. One that hurt. What did she say to her mother? That marriage and family hadn't made her mother happy? She couldn't say the words. Couldn't stand the distance between her parents and knew there was no way for her to fix it. That it couldn't be fixed.

"Gramma's asking for you, Mom." Kendra came to the rescue, breezing in to sweep her baby daughter from Kristin's arms. "Oh, she likes her auntie Kristin."

"The feeling's mutual." Kristin stroked Caitlin's soft cheek, careful not to wake the drowsing infant. "She's pretty great."

"Cam and I think so, too." Kendra beamed with the quiet glow of happiness, and Kristin wondered about that as she watched her mom and sister retreat to the warm kitchen, where the women in the family gathered.

This was her favorite part of the holidays. In the flurry of activity in preparing the meal, for one moment, the family felt whole. Undiminished. Michelle laugh-

ing as she teased Karen about her latest shoe faux pas,
Kirby whipping the potatoes and stopping midway
through to search through the kitchen for more butter.
Karen teasing Michelle back when a carrot coin rolled
off the center island and onto her shoe. Kendra, with
babe on her hip, digging the condiments out of the back
of the fridge. Gramma bemoaning the lumps in her
gravy that didn't exist, interspersed with the disorgan-
ized discussion of the latest family news.

Dad ambled into the women's domain in his only
good red-and-black flannel shirt and brown jeans. Quiet
as always, he searched through the drawers for the carv-
ing knife.

"It's right there on the counter." Mom's tight words
broke the magic, and the cheer faded.

Dad picked up the knife and went to work slicing the
waiting turkey, and Gramma tried to heal the awkward
silence by complimenting Mom on the perfect turkey.

Kristin took the covered wrap off the fruit salad and
sunk a serving spoon into the sweet froth of whipped
cream, sliced apples and bananas and carried it and the
serving dish of jellied cranberries to the table. She wondered how Ryan was faring. Better, she hoped.

Images of him whisked through her mind. Was his
first Thanksgiving at home since he'd graduated as
happy as it should be? Surely this hardworking man
with values and integrity, who had undoubtedly saved
the accident victim's life, deserved one good day. At the
very least.

She set the bottles and bowl on the table. Why was

she thinking about Ryan? She liked him. She wished him well. But it wasn't as if she'd see him again. Why would she? Their paths would never cross again.

She couldn't say why that made her so sad, but it did. It felt like another loss that didn't fade but lingered as she returned to the kitchen, where the strain between her mom and dad was as unmistakable as the floor at her feet.

He was suffocating as sure as if his lungs had collapsed. Ryan took a long pull of the cherry soda Mom had dug out of the back of the refrigerator, from behind her bowls of salad and cranberry jelly and the covered plates of homemade fudge. The bubbly sweetness chased down his throat but didn't help him breathe any better.

Snow was starting to tumble from a peaceful sky, falling in a hush. With the pop of the woodstove and squeak and bang of the open door and Mom's cheerful hum as she checked on the turkey in the oven, he couldn't hear the quiet reverence that came. But it was there just the same. The world quieted, as if just to hear the fragile tap, tap, tap of snowflakes on the earth.

Heaven must be like this, Dad had said once, on their early Sunday-morning forays into the wilderness. Ryan nudged aside the ruffled edge of the frilly curtains to gaze out at the tree line.

If he looked hard enough there was the past, alive within him, as he remembered the cold creeping through the layers of wool Mom had wrapped him up in. Snow crept over the top of his high boots to wet his pant legs tucked inside, and melted as it slid down to his ankle.

There was a cadence to the falling snow, and he, like nature surrounding him, leaned forward, holding his breath to hear it. Feel it. The reverence of the hills, as if relaxing to accept their mantle of snow. The mountains rising like awed worshipers, their faces lost in the mist and clouds.

Everywhere, the land felt at peace, as if at prayer, and Ryan had felt it, too. The stroke of God's hand in everything, and then Dad's low baritone, rumbling low out of respect for the Maker, as he leaned close.

"I've always thought that heaven would feel like this, solemn and awesome and so beautiful it makes your eyes water to look at it."

Ryan cleared his throat, looking away, setting the half-empty soda can on the edge of the counter. Too many emotions. He'd worked most of his life not to remember. Not to feel. Like ice cracking beneath the snow, pain splintered inside his chest.

"Oh, that was Alice." Mom set down the cordless handset he hadn't noticed she'd even picked up. "She loved my recipe for cranberry jelly. She said it was much better than the recipe she'd used last year. It was the hit of their Thanksgiving dinner."

"We had a bet going. I told her if she didn't just love it, then I'd treat her to lunch. It's a new recipe I found in one of those fancy cooking magazines, and oh, it's a winner." Mom beamed with a steady happiness as she brushed lustrous strands of hair out of her eyes. "Oh, it's so *good* to see you standing in my kitchen."

"It's kinda good to be here, too." Okay, here it came. The mushy part. He braced himself. He wasn't one to let his defenses down. He opened his arms and let her walk into them. Let her squeeze him in a bear hug. Warmth glowed inside him, melting away the pain. But love came with its own pain.

"I love my little mom," he said to make her laugh.

She stepped away to look up at him. "How did my little boy get to be so big?"

"Remember those vitamins you made me eat with breakfast every morning? They worked."

"I see that." Tears gleamed in her eyes, eyes that were wise and kind and a beautiful hazel-green. In them, he saw her pleasure at having him home, and noticed something else. No more shadows. She was finally at peace.

She'd worked so hard for them. For him.

Time looped back on itself, in the fluid way of memories, and he saw the kitchen of his youth. The yellowed linoleum floors and the ancient cabinet doors that wouldn't stay shut but would swing open whenever the mood suited them. The red countertop worn white in places from several decades of wipe downs and dripping dishes drying in a rack beneath the window. Mom, hollow-eyed with exhaustion as she worked, humming away to make their meager Thanksgiving Day meal a feast.

It wasn't the poverty that had ever bothered him. It

wasn't the odd jobs he worked for the neighbors to bring in cash to help out, before he'd been old enough to be hired on at the grocery. None of that really mattered. It was the deep yearning for his dad.

If only he could have one more day. Just one more day of wading through the knee-deep snow and listening to the music of snowfall alongside the man who'd always been so tall, seemed so big and strong and everything good in a man. Invincible.

I miss you, Dad.

The ice shards in his chest seemed to splinter into more sharp blades stabbing into his heart. If he let it, it was a pain that could drown him until there was nothing else. He fought it by shutting off his feelings.

"My, it gives me a start to see you standing there." Mom had turned from checking on the progress of something on the stove, one hand clutching the neck of her shirt. "You look so much like him. Like your father. It's takes me back to when he was alive and standing in my kitchen. Right there at the window, like you are now…"

Don't go there, Mom. The thought blared in his mind, but he didn't dare open his mouth to speak. He couldn't take any more memories.

"…with shoulders so broad and strong, I felt as if he could handle anything. That nothing would ever hurt me as long as he was there." Mom's words resounded with true love, like a candlelight hymn, but they bore wounds in his heart as surely as if they'd been bullets blasting into his flesh.

He turned away, thinking of last night's blizzard and how it had shrouded him from the rest of the world. He made himself like that, steeling the walls of his heart.

Mom kept talking, but he wouldn't listen. He just couldn't let her in. He was like a drowning man going down for the last time. Feeling the icy waters welling up from within, he prayed for relief.

As if the angels heard and took pity on him, his cell chirped. His E.R. doc buddy Tim's number flashed on the phone's small screen. You'd better have good news, man, Ryan thought. Because right now he couldn't take any more bad news.

Chapter Six

Kristin entered the post-Thanksgiving dinner calm of the unoccupied dining room, slid the Monopoly box onto the table and sank into a cushioned chair. Yawning from too much turkey, she could put her feet up and sneak in a nap—yeah, as if her sisters were going to let her get away with that.

She could hear their voices throughout the house. Karen and Kirby in the kitchen talking about the family's beloved pony, Honeybear, which they'd all learned to ride on and now was teaching a second generation of McKaslin girls. Their laughter rose higher and fell below the hum of the dishwasher and the clink of pots as they put the last of the hand-washed dishes away.

Kendra, who kept the pony at her riding stable, chimed in with a comment Kristin couldn't quite make out as the roar of the football game in the living room rose into a frenzied crescendo. It wouldn't feel like a holiday without Dad glued to the big-screen TV he'd splurged on and his muttering commentary on the referee's call was a sound she'd heard every game day since she was little.

It was good to know some things would never change. That's what got her through the sadness of sitting at this table where Gramma occupied Allison's chair, which had remained empty for years. With the leaves in the center, the table stretched to nearly fill the entire room. There were so many of them with the additions to their family—her sisters' husbands and kids. It was a good thing she'd decided not to ever get married. Because there would be no room for another man at the table!

Oh, it's good to be home. Kristin breathed deep, and the warm scents of this day soothed her. The spicy goodness of Gramma's pumpkin pie warming in the oven. The vanilla candles she'd gotten Mom last Christmas burning with a cheery brightness in the corner by the window. The steady comfort of brewing coffee seasoning the air.

She rubbed at the tension in the back of her neck. Wow, her muscles were knotted up good. It was always this way. Allison's loss was like a layer of ice over a cold pond of grief. No matter how many layers of snow covered it, no matter how hard her family tried to reach for that contented wholeness that used to exist, the ice was there. The loss. There was no solid place to stand on.

Youngest sister, Michelle, glowing in the second trimester of pregnancy, padded out from the kitchen with a bowl of rippled potato chips and stacked covered bowls of different flavors of homemade dip. She unloaded them on the table. "There's no place like home, is there?"

"Nope. It's good to be back."

"This house used to be so lonely. You know…after Allison." Michelle peeled back the plastic wrap from the first bowl of dip. "But not anymore. Good changes, don't you think?"

It was the same—the house, the sense of family and the feeling of home. But time had changed the details, added texture. Little kids ran around the living room, now scattered with colorful plastic toys. A baby drowsed in her swing, her blond curls glistening.

Kristin leaned just enough to see through the archway into the living room. The back of Dad's head, his hair thinning and graying, was visible over the back of the couch. But he wasn't alone. Gramma's new husband, Willard, had claimed the recliner. Michelle's and Kendra's husbands flanked Dad on either side. Karen's and Kirby's husbands took up the sectional in the corner.

It was weird to think all her sisters had married. Were wives and mothers.

And mothers-to-be.

"You have another good change coming." Kristin nodded toward Michelle's thickening waist.

"I know! Gabe and I weren't planning a second child so soon, but, oops!" Michelle stole a chip from the heaping bowl and crunched on it. "During the ultrasound, we accidentally found out if we're having a boy or a girl. No, I'm not going to tell you. It'll, like, ruin the surprise for everyone else."

"How am I going to know what color stuff to buy for your shower?"

"Ooh, and you buy good stuff, too. You're the only sister I have with any fashion sense at all. If I give you a hint, then it's not like really telling."

"Exactly. I'm a great secret keeper. You know that."

Michelle pushed a lock of hair behind her ear and stole another chip. "Let's just say I'm not going to be able to use Emily's baby things for this little one. I'm going to need all new stuff."

That could only mean one thing. A little nephew was on the way. "Michelle. Lucky you. Congratulations."

"Thanks. I am pretty lucky."

There was no mistaking her happiness. Now. But what about down the road?

Troubled, Kristin grabbed a bowl and flicked off the plastic wrap. "Hmm, French onion. Gramma's secret recipe. I'm glad some things never change."

"The best stuff just keeps getting better, don't you think?"

"Yeah. I know what you mean." For all her sadness, there was gratitude, too, for the blessings surrounding her. Home and family, health and hope. Everything good in her life was because she'd grown up here, because of the people in this house.

Michelle lifted the tattered lid of their old Monopoly box. "Kirby and Karen are planning on rounding up the kids and bedding them down in my old room. Once everyone's napping, we'll get started. Sound like a plan?"

"A good one. Are the husbands going to join us, or will it be just us girls?"

"Hmm. Let me think." Michelle turned to study the strapping men clustered around the television, leaning forward, attention one hundred percent on the game. The big screen showed the quarterback passing the ball to a wide receiver, and the men leaped to their feet, shouting and cheering.

The baby woke up and sniffled.

"Hmm, I don't think we should let dudes who act like that near us," Michelle decided with a twinkle as she went to rescue her little one in the swing.

"Good decision."

Kristin considered her brothers-in-law. They all seemed like good men. She hardly knew them, having spent bits and pieces of time with them through her visits home. What mattered to her was how those men treated her sisters. As long as her sisters were happy, then she liked her brothers-in-law just fine.

But marriage was marriage—inevitably love faded, problems and hardship broke the best of relationships. Diminished the greatest romance. Men let women down; yeah, she got that. That's why she was way too smart to ever get married. To put that much trust in anyone. Sisters were one thing. They had bonds that would never break.

But romantic love was a whole different story—*that*

kind of love was like a fragile bloom on the hard Montana plains. Short-lived and quick to wither in the bitter north winds.

A movement caught her eye. A man's broad-shouldered shadow fell across the snow in front of the picture window. That profile sure looked familiar. The doorbell rang, although it was hard to hear above the noise of the cranked-up TV and the men shouting like the crazed fans they were in the living room. She alone seemed to notice the visitor's silhouette against the etched glass in the door.

Kristin yanked open the door, glad to see Ryan Sanders blocking the porch light, snow glistening in his dark hair. "Hey, what are you doing here? You clean up real nice."

"Right. Oh, I shaved." He ran one hand along his square jaw. "I bring good news and the fudge my mom promised your mom but didn't get a chance to drop by. She said since I was coming over, I'd better not come empty-handed. I need something to bribe my way through the door."

"We don't let your kind in otherwise."

When he laughed, dimples framed his smile. He had a great smile, the kind that lit him up from within. And it made Kristin feel bright inside, too. She took the offered tin, topped with an amber-and-orange ribbon.

She breathed in the fudgy aroma. "Hmm, my mouth is already watering. Your mom makes the best fudge in three states. Did you want to come in? Or are you just dropping this by? Did you hear about Samantha?"

"I did. God must have heard your prayers because Tim told me they took a bone spur out of her neck, between C2 and C3 vertebrae. The bone didn't penetrate her spinal cord, and except for a little swelling against the nerve roots, she's fine."

"And does that mean she's going to be all right?"

"Yeah. They pinned a broken bone in her lower right leg, turned out to be a fracture, but other than that, she's fine. Considering the cold, it could have been a lot worse. It's a good thing we came along when we did."

It was no coincidence. The certainty of it steadied her. The long events of the last night had happened for a reason. What if Ryan hadn't flown into Seattle for his job interview? Then he would never have been on the flight that was diverted to Boise. And if not for the storm, then he wouldn't have been anywhere near the lonely stretch of road where Samantha Fields had crashed. As the Good Lord would have it, Ryan, a doctor, was there to help when he was needed. He made a true difference in the world.

"Is that football?" Ryan leaned past her to sneak a look at the game in full-color glory on the wide screen. "Man, look at that TV."

"It's Dad's pride and joy. Don't tell me you like football."

"Like it? It's only like the most important thing in the world." He rolled his eyes, which sparkled with humor. "How could you not know that?"

"My mistake. Sorry. Football ranks right above world peace. I should have known. You're welcome to come inside and watch the game."

"Thanks. Ooh, a fumble!" Ryan's groan matched the series of painful noises rising up in the living room.

"Come in. Stay. There's probably room for you on the floor in the corner. We won't charge you admission *this* time, since you're a friend of the family and all."

"Kristin, you're fabulous. You know that, right? It's been killin' me not being able to see this game. Mom's satellite is out." He took a step forward, enough to see the replay of his team's fumble. "That's killin' me, too."

"Take off your coat before you go gawk at the TV." She held out her hand.

But Ryan, all his attention focused on the game, shrugged out of his black leather jacket and went to snag it on the coat tree all by himself—and missed. He got it on the second try.

Kristin closed the door against the gentle drift of snow. What was it about men and football? "Do you want something to drink? We've got soda, coffee or juice."

"Soda, if it's not too much trouble." He flashed her a wink, friendly and easy, not flirty at all.

Then why did her toes tingle? That was certainly the wrong response. She was not interested in him at all. *Not in the slightest.* So, why wouldn't her toes stop tingling as she sashayed into the kitchen, slid the fudge on the counter and plundered a can of cola from the crowded fridge.

Mom looked up from the corner table where she was sitting with Gramma and doing needlework. She looked far too, well, innocent. As if she was incredibly surprised by the simple tin on the counter. "Goodness! Is that Mary's fudge? Why, was that her at the door?"

"No, her son is in our living room right now." Kristin didn't have to turn around. She already knew what Mom was going to say next. "Yeah, I know he's a doctor and I know he's an eligible bachelor. But I'm not *interested.*" She enunciated very clearly so Mom couldn't misunderstand.

Her mother was clearly plotting. There was no way she was going to believe that Ryan just *happened* to come over today, of all days, when the two of them had driven up together in the same car. No, Mom had been on the phone with Mary earlier. "You're not going to fool me, Mother dear. I know Mary sent him over and the two of you are hoping we'll fall madly in love and get married."

"Married? Why, of course not. What ever gave you that idea?"

Kirby looked up from counting out the good dessert plates from the china cabinet. "Gee, I wonder. Maybe I heard you tell Mary it was a sign from above, the two of them bumping into each other at the airport. Then you suggested that Mary send her son over today, so the kids could get better acquainted."

"Why, we were talking about the fudge. Surely you misunderstood." But Mom looked way too pleased with herself. "But since you brought up the subject, then yes. What Kristin needs is to find a nice doctor like Ryan."

"Mom!" Kristin groaned.

"Mom!" Karen protested.

"Mother!" Kirby chimed in a lighthearted reprimand. "Let Kristin find her own man. I have perfect faith she'll find the right one."

"Thanks." How she loved her sisters. There was nothing like solidarity. "Maybe I don't want a nice doctor."

"Yeah, Mom, maybe Kristin wants a mean doctor." Kendra spoke up from slicing pie at the counter.

"Any old doctor will do," Kristin added, kidding.

"Yeah," oldest sister Karen agreed as she uncapped a pitcher of Gramma's lemon-lime punch. "We wouldn't want our dear Kristin to take her time and find a loving and strong man. No, we want her to take any old guy who comes along. So what if he's mean? Or lazy? Or can't keep a job?"

"Yeah, Mom." Michelle tugged out clean forks and knives from the silent dishwasher. "Kristin would be married. *That's* what matters. So what if it's to the wrong guy. It isn't the guy that's important. It's the wedding ring. Right?"

"Oh, you girls!" Mom chuckled as she pulled her embroidery thread tight. "All right, you win. I'll stop."

"Stop?" Kristin wasn't fooled. "No, you'll never stop. You'll just cease to harp on my getting married for about two minutes. *Maybe.*"

"Two minutes?" Karen piled a thick wedge of pie on a dessert plate. "Do you think Mom can hold out that long? I say a minute and a half."

"One minute." Gramma set down her crocheting and held up her wrist to stare at her gold watch.

Mom pretended to look shocked. "You are all exaggerating. I do not harp."

"Yes, you do, Mom." Kirby's gentle ribbing included wrapping their mother in a big hug. "Admit it."

"Yeah, admit it, Mom." Kristin set down the glass and soda can and wrapped her arms around Mom and Kirby. "It's the second thing you talk about every time you call, right after 'hello.' You say, 'have you met anyone yet?'"

"I'm not that bad."

"You're *that* bad." Kendra was next, joining the circle.

Followed by Karen. "We like our Kristin happy and we want her to stay that way, married or not."

Kristin leaned her cheek against Karen's. What would she do without her sisters?

Michelle entered the room with a distressed cry. "Like, leave me out!" She joined the circle with outstretched arms.

Boots knelled on the linoleum and stopped. "All right, break it up. What does a man have to do to get a drink around here?"

Ryan. Kristin took a step back, unaware of her sisters milling around. Mom's warm greeting buzzed like a fly next to her ear. Yep, by the sound of it, Mom was definitely hoping for a match between them.

She knew her mother meant well, but please! She held up the glass. "I wasn't about to let you dehydrate. I know you have to keep your throat well lubricated for all that yelling you men do at the refs and the players."

"And the coaches. Thanks." Ryan took the glass. "I can remember the last time I've been in your kitchen. I think it was the summer I turned eight and Mom made me go everywhere with her."

"Wasn't that the summer you drove the family car into the ditch?"

"Yep. Not one of my better moments. I was just pretending to drive. How was I to know the parking brake wouldn't hold? I popped in the clutch and the car rolled backward down the driveway and into the irrigation ditch."

Her sisters' laughter filled the air. "I remember," Karen began. "Dad drove the tractor over to pull the car out."

"You were the talk of the church picnic the next day," Kirby added. "No one figured you'd wreck the family sedan before you hit your teens."

"Mom grounded me for life after that. She commuted my sentence to three weeks when the same thing happened to her and she dented Mr. Winkler's Buick. Seems the parking brake really *was* faulty so she got it fixed."

Ryan couldn't believe it. The McKaslin girls may have grown up and gotten married, were wives and mothers, but they were still the same—warm, friendly and lighthearted.

It had been a long time since he'd felt this at-home anywhere. Obeying the demands of his rumbling stomach, he flicked off the lid and took a big fat gooey piece of fudge. "Karen, Kendra, Kirby. It's good to see you again. And little Michelle, look at you. When are you due?"

"This spring. This one will be my second. Emily's in the living room with her daddy." Beaming, Michelle stroked her sizable stomach and stopped to listen. "I hear more groans coming from the living room. Bad news?"

"Painful. That's why I'm here. Thought I'd hide from the grim sight of my lifelong favorite team getting thrashed. Figured the sight of you beautiful ladies would help ease the sting of defeat."

"That compliment earns you a piece of the pie of your choice." Kristin, by far the most beautiful of the sisters, held out two plates. "Apple or pumpkin?"

Was that real whipped cream? Yep, it looked like the real thing. As genuine and rich as the woman in front of him. "Are you kidding? It's Thanksgiving. Pumpkin."

Mrs. McKaslin leaned over the table to say, in that way of matchmaking mothers, "Kristin is an excellent baker. Aren't you, sweetie?"

"I'm the worst baker of the group and you know it." Kristin turned a cute shade of pink. Embarrassed, she jabbed a fork at him, taking the slice of apple pie over to her mom. "You promised to stop."

"Yes, but he's a *doctor*."

Poor Kristin. She looked so exasperated and embarrassed. He had lots of practice with this subject. "If I had a buck every time I heard a woman's mother say that, I'd have my med-school loans paid off by now. I know. Marrying off your daughters is a mother's duty."

"That it is. I want all of my girls happy."

"*Mom.* I'm happy the way I am." Kristin marched the length of the kitchen, keeping far away from him.

She wasn't even giving him those telling looks, the ones that said that she was hoping for a doctor to marry and zeroing in on him, since he was single.

After yanking open the freezer, she dropped a gallon of Neapolitan ice cream on the counter with a resounding thud. "Don't take this personally, Ryan. Mom has had so much fun planning everyone's wedding, that she wants to plan mine next."

"Oh, I understand. Believe me. It was my mom who conveniently 'forgot' to bring the fudge by."

"I know your pain." Kristin looked a little less embarrassed. "Ice cream?"

"With my second piece of pie, sure. Let me finish this one first."

"What makes you think that you get seconds?"

"My charming personality?" That made everyone laugh. Okay, so he liked being the center of attention. Who didn't? And it felt good to be accepted so easily into the McKaslins' family circle, when his mom's house offered him no peace.

"All right, Mr. Charming. Make yourself useful and take that with you." Kristin shoved two dessert plates at him. Huge pie wedges topped with scoops of vanilla and chocolate. "The apple's for Dad. The other is for whoever grabs it first."

"Me, useful? You've got the wrong impression of me. I'm never useful."

"Never. *Right*." Sparkling with held-back laughter, Kristin breezed away, taking with her the scent of vanilla and something else. He couldn't name it as he hesitated.

He didn't want to leave just yet. There was something troubling him. Something within him that wanted to stay in the light of her presence. "Anything else I can carry for you, while I'm here?"

"Nope. That's it." Her eyes danced as she studied him from behind the refrigerator door.

An odd sensation tightened deep within his chest. The ice within him cracked, and that hurt, too, although he didn't know why. Maybe because he stood in the kitchen of a real family. One with both parents. He'd always admired the McKaslins. In truth, when he'd been young, been envious of them, too. Not that he was proud of it, but he'd learned since then that the grass is always greener on the other side of the fence.

Although, standing in this kitchen looked pretty great to him. Since that was way too domestic of a thought for a guy like him, Ryan trained his attention on the living room. Exit stage left.

"I'm getting out of here before I eat *all* the pie." He caught Kristin's twinkling gaze as he left the room, leaving the women laughing behind him.

He handed off the pie plates and took the corner of the couch. That TV sure was something. He could see every detail with perfection as his team lined up on the thirty-four, third down and five to go. They were behind, okay, so they were losing, but if they made a good play, they had a good chance to—

"Yeah!" Shouts rose around him, Zach and Sam, two of the brothers-in-law, jumped to their feet, urging the running back on. The twenty-two, the eighteen—"Keep goin', c'mon!"

Down at the fifteen. Ryan was on his feet. Excitement zinged through him. He shoveled down pie, along with the other men in the room during the huddle, which took forever. When he should have been willing his quarterback to pass, his thoughts were not on the game. But on the golden-haired woman, her short hair sweeping against her jaw as she circled around the couch and into the dining room.

The team broke up, warriors hungry for victory.

"Run it," Mr. McKaslin advised.

"A pass, high and long," Sam, Kirby's husband, shouted at the screen.

"No, all they need is a field goal," Zach argued.

The center hiked the ball. Ryan's fork froze in mid-air as he watched the play unfold. A sack attempt by the defense, but the quarterback feigned right in time, stepped left and arced the ball with the perfect spin to set it in the tailback's hands behind the goal line. Touchdown!

Ryan yelled right along with the others. Yeah! They had a chance of winning this one. Something buzzed at the back of his neck. He slapped his hand there—not a bug or an itch or anything. The tickle remained. When he looked up, Kristin was in his line of sight, unboxing a board game on the dining-room table.

She sure was nice. He'd noticed that before—but not

like this. Never like this. On the plane she'd looked coolly professional in her power suit. On the long drive through Idaho, she'd looked in charge and competent. Everything he'd expect in an urban woman with, as his mom always put it, a highfalutin' job. He'd liked that Kristin.

He liked this one more. She was one hundred percent pure Montana girl in worn jeans and a gray U of M sweatshirt. Girl-next-door fresh and warmhearted. Deep in his chest his steel defenses buckled a little, letting in a crack in the armor. Giving way to a hitch of emotion, but he shut that down before the feeling could grow.

His cell chirped from the entryway. Taking the pie with him, he wolfed down the last of the rich spicy pumpkin as he dashed through the room and down the hall. He dug out the phone and flipped it open. "Hey, Mom."

"I hope you're not ruining your appetite."

"How do you always know when I'm misbehaving? Not only do you have eyes in the back of your head but you have X-ray vision, too."

"Of course! Mothers are extraordinary, my boy. Besides, I can tell you're talking with your mouth full. My bet is pie."

"And it's good pie."

"Not one more piece, young man! The turkey comes out of the oven in twenty minutes, and I want you front and center to carve it for me. Oh! Your sister just drove up. I've got to go."

"I'm on my way," he promised, snapping off the phone.

Home. His guts tightened. Tension snaked through his muscles and he realized he was holding his breath.

Time to go home. To face again the house that brought back memories that could make him bleed.

He felt her presence behind him, knew it was Kristin before he turned with his coat over his arm. "My mom said I have to go home now. It's dinnertime. It's funny. I haven't said those words since I was eighteen."

"Ah, that's what you get for coming home. No matter how old you are, you're still your parents' kid."

"Yeah." He felt awkward. He didn't know why.

Maybe it was because he didn't want to face the past, or maybe it was that he didn't want to leave this house full of love and family togetherness. Of easy laughter and unfailing devotion. He simply didn't want to leave just yet and Kristin was the reason. The pretty woman with the shadows in her expressive eyes and the amazing blend of honest country girl and successful career woman.

Haloed in the soft illumination of the wall sconce, she seemed to softly glow. Her hair shimmered with a hundred different shades of gold, and light burnished her shoulders so that when she reached out to take his plate, she was the most beautiful image he'd ever seen.

Her hands were slender and fine-boned with beautifully tapered fingers. Her nails were short and painted a seashell pink. It looked as if hers would be a nice hand to hold in his.

Not that he was looking for wife candidates. He was deeply committed to his bachelor status. Still, she was sure something, as if the light moved through her and he could see her goodness. Her kindness. He swallowed past the sudden tightness in his throat and shrugged into his jacket. "Take good care of yourself, Kristin McKaslin."

"You, too, Dr. Sanders."

The next step he took felt like a momentous one. As if he'd reached a fork in his life path offering two very different choices. It was a weird way to feel, because there was nothing consequential about opening the door and walking into the snow. Nothing life changing about zipping up his zipper and digging the keys out of his jeans pocket.

Then why did it feel wrong, somehow? When his mom was waiting for him, and his sister was probably chatting a hundred miles a minute in the kitchen. In twenty minutes he'd be sitting down for Thanksgiving dinner.

His feelings didn't make sense. Not at all.

He was just troubled about being here in Montana. Maybe that was it. As he crunched down the snowy steps and the winter air radiated through his coat to make him shiver, no other explanation came to mind. Only four more hours, he thought, glancing at his watch. His flight departed at seven-thirty—the airport had recovered from the blizzard and was up and running. He could survive until then.

As he drove off, the day was already changing. Twilight cast a somber mood across the snow-mantled world. Making the shadows a deep blue-gray and the sky a mourning shroud as memories, cold and dark, had a hold on him and didn't let go.

Chapter Seven

December 3

With the temperate heat of the Phoenix sun on his back, Ryan pushed hard for the last quarter mile. Jogging wasn't his favorite thing—it made his shins hurt, his knees ache and it was plain hard work—but for some unexplained reason he looked forward to setting out on his five-mile run every day after work. Even on a perfect Saturday like this one.

Not a cloud in the bright blue sky. The sun a friendly brightness reflecting off the miles of concrete and pavement that comprised the Scottsdale neighborhood he lived in. All different kinds of palm trees, from the short stubby pineapple palms to the tall tropical ones, waved their fronds in the breeze.

His neighbor's cat darted out from beneath the oleander hedges and streaked down the sidewalk and out of sight. Nothing but a blur of gray and white. Tonight, as usual, he'd terrify the poor animal, without meaning to, by opening his slider door.

The cat napped on Ryan's lounge-chair cushion. Not that he minded, but he would rather befriend the animal instead of always watching it run in the opposite direction.

He understood, though. He and that cat had a lot in common. Keep your distance. Don't trust anyone.

He was so good, he'd perfected it into an art form.

At the end of the hedges, he dropped into a walk. Sweat sluiced off him, but it felt good to have pushed like that. He worked indoors all day. He loved his work; he just hated being confined.

Probably because he'd spent most of his youth outside—playing in the meadows and woods, riding his bike for miles on quiet country roads and, when he was older, working in the fields for extra money. Throughout the long years of his medical training, he'd spent endless hours indoors. He'd never acclimated to it.

It had gotten worse since he'd been back home for Thanksgiving.

Scottsdale had its own strange beauty. Not the rugged granite mountains and lush fertile river valley of his hometown. Still, the eerily human forms of the saguaro cacti, with their arms stretched toward heaven, and the stubborn green of the palm trees and the rocky camelback ridges of the Superstition Mountains were a form of beauty, too.

It just wasn't Montana.

Ryan wasn't sure if it was Montana he missed or the

woman he'd reunited with there. Kristin had been on his mind since he'd left the McKaslins' home to carve Mom's turkey. He didn't know why he kept thinking about her. Probably because she was really something, that's why. Just because he planned on being unattached forever didn't mean he couldn't appreciate a fine woman.

It didn't help matters that Mom had done nothing else but talk up Kristin. Through their Thanksgiving meal, Mom kept peppering the conversation with comments about Kristin, even if she had to change the subject back to the pretty Montana girl. She was so successful that she'd bought her own place. She was smart with money. She wasn't dating anyone. She had a lot in common with him. She loved movies and books and she jogged, too.

Poor Mom. He knew it was hard for her to understand why he stayed single. That really perplexed him because she'd lost Dad, too. She'd never dated. She'd never considered getting remarried. So, why did she want him to? Both of them knew there was no sense in going through that kind of pain again. People died. Life ended. As a doctor, he couldn't deny how frail life was.

He wasn't about to get close to anyone again. No. He couldn't take that kind of devastation one more time. He was just fine alone. It hadn't been easy for the eight-year-old he'd been to attend his dad's funeral. To try to pick up the pieces shattering all around him—his mom's grief, his own heartbreak, the gaping hole that Dad had left behind. To live every day without him, to comfort his mom and sister, to worry about money, to know that if he lost one parent, then he could just as easily, just as suddenly, lose the other.

No, he'd lived with enough of that uncertainty. Swiping the sweat from his brow, he stopped in front of the mailboxes and bent down to give his hamstrings a good stretch. He'd missed a few days of running, with the holidays and the long office hours. He was paying for it now.

He looked in his mailbox—the standard stuff. The water bill. Pizza ads. A flyer for free windshield-crack repairs. And a bonus—an envelope from Tim, his buddy in Boise. The E.R. doc. Ryan ripped that one open.

"Hey, Ryan," he read in Tim's typical hurried, doctor's scrawl. "Samantha Fields was discharged last week, and she asked me to pass these notes on to you. I didn't know the woman you were with, but I figure you'll know how to reach her."

Ryan looked in the envelope at the two note cards, one addressed to him and the other simply to Kristin.

There he was, thinking about her again. How there'd been steel in her that night—how she'd worked without complaint in the bitter cold to help him tend to Samantha. And there was light in her, the kind that shone as true as the sun. A kindness that moved even a grouchy old bachelor like him, who was so set in his ways.

The trouble was, he didn't have her address in Seattle. If he called his mom, boy, would she make a big deal about it. She'd think she was making progress on her campaign to match him up with a suitable woman. No, he couldn't call his mom. A call to Kristin's mom was out, too.

One of her sisters. Yeah, he'd give Kirby a call. Kirby was a nurse. She understood about confidentiality. He'd get her number from information. Yep, that was a good idea. This way his mom would never know he wanted to write Kristin.

It wasn't his idea to write her, after all. Nope. It was his duty to forward the note from Samantha Fields. And, being an honorable man, what else could he do?

December 8

Rain smeared the windshield of Kristin's sedan and the wipers couldn't keep up with the downpour. Water rushed in rivulets down the paved city streets and sheened on the blacktop of her complex's parking lot. It was only seven o'clock, but it could have been midnight, for the evening felt bleak and endless.

She hit her garage-door opener, grateful to be home safe. The freeway through the downtown corridor had been a mess. Accidents everywhere, lanes of traffic idling in both directions for miles. She turned off the engine, clicked off the headlights, gathered up her work and hit the garage-door button. With the wind and cold locked safely outside, she hopped up the three steps to her kitchen door and unlocked it.

Two frowning Persian cats were two shadows of fluffy shades of gray in the middle of the kitchen. They studied her with unblinking eyes. *Uh-oh, there was a reprimand coming.*

"I'm late, I know. I'm sorry." She dropped her armload of work on the counter, along with her purse, and shrugged out of her waterproof coat.

The garment was still a little damp from her run from the office building to the parking garage—the economical parking was down the street, of course, she didn't want to pay a premium just to park close—but today she'd regretted her sensible budgeting. She'd been soaked the instant she stepped outside. Lovely. She was still wet through. And cold.

The dripping water was another transgression to the cats that had obvious standards to maintain. They still hadn't entirely forgiven her for leaving them for Thanksgiving.

"I know it's hard being inside in the warm house all day." She knelt to thread her fingers through the warm silk of their fluffy hair. Minnie, who held a grudge the longest, looked away, but Mickey, her brother, leaned into Kristin's touch and gave a gravelly purr.

"I missed you, too." She loved animals. She'd never been without a pet of one kind or another until she'd left home for college. As soon as she had her own place, she'd bought the pair of kittens, who'd been the best company. A little demanding, but then, cats were very wise and regal creatures.

She refilled their water bowls and Mickey's dish was low on dry food, so she filled that, too. Shivering, she turned up the heat as she hurried through the living room. It was a small place, but cozy, with a wide bay-window seat near the front door and a gas fireplace in the back wall.

Even though she'd lived here for two years, she was still fixing it up, according to her budget. She'd taken a week of vacation in October and had painted the living room a soft butter yellow. On cold dark nights like this one, the walls glowed with soft warmth.

She'd reupholstered the matching couches in amber tweed that matched the walls. When she took a few extra days after Christmas, she was going to refinish the built-in bookcases packed with hundreds of paperbacks that filled three of the four walls from floor to ceiling.

The TV tucked in the corner was tuned to the one that seemed to interest the cats—the Discovery Channel. Kristin grabbed the remote off the coffee table she'd picked out with last year's Christmas money from Gramma and flipped through the cable listings until she found a beloved Doris Day movie.

Minnie flicked her tail and hopped onto the arm of the couch. Daintily picking up her tiny, soft downy paws, she settled on the back of the cushion and made an adorable fluffy ball. The feline eyed Doris Day swimming around in a mermaid's costume with clear disapproval.

Next trip home, Kristin decided, she was definitely taking the cats with her.

Thoughts of Montana naturally led to memories of Thanksgiving and of Ryan Sanders—of how he'd changed into a man to admire.

It was a no-brainer that Mom had turned his visit on Thanksgiving into a major deal. Every time Mom called since, she'd mentioned something she'd heard about him, through Mary. How busy he was, that he'd just bought a new car, how he'd taken a weekend and gone skiing in New Mexico with some of his doctor buddies. "What he really needs," Mom had confided, "is a wife. Mary worries about him."

If there was anyone who could take care of himself, it was Dr. Ryan Sanders. As she unlocked the door and stepped out onto the covered front step to grab her mail from the little white box, she wondered if she'd ever met anyone more competent. She'd never forget how he'd handled the emergency that night—his hands so steady, his actions so controlled, his calm wisdom.

Why did she sigh when she thought of him? It wasn't as if she was interested in him.

She slammed the door shut against the damp night and stood over the heat register, shivering. A letter from Gramma. She'd save that to read while she ate. A reminder from the state vehicle people that her license tabs needed to be renewed. Oh, and a letter from…she squinted at the strange names of the return address etched in gold. A law office? No, a doctor's office. In Arizona.

Ryan! She ripped the envelope open and she didn't care if she was way too eager. They were, well, sort of friends. It was always good to hear from a friend, right?

Dear Kristin.

It was hard to read his block letters, his handwriting was more of a scribble. So she sat down on the corner of the couch and switched on the table lamp.

Our patient has made a full recovery and is back
at school. I don't know if I ever thanked you for
everything that night. You were really something.
Thanks. I still owe you for driving through daybreak so I could sleep. Since Mom has twisted my
arm and made me promise to come home for
Christmas, I've actually got more than the one
day off. I get the entire weekend, too, so what do
you say I treat you to milkshakes at The Sunshine Café? You name the time and the date, and
I'll be there.

Milkshakes? She laughed, amazed that he'd remembered they'd discussed chocolate milkshakes as they'd
driven through town Thanksgiving morning.

P.S. Samantha sent this to me.

Inside the envelope was a sealed note card—a note
from Samantha Fields.

Dear Kristin, I can't believe how blessed I am to
have been rescued by you and Ryan. I just wanted
to thank you for helping me. God bless you.

It was signed, Sam.
Wow. Of course, Ryan was the one who'd made the
real difference, being the doctor. He'd known just what
to do to help minimize Sam's injuries. Yeah, he was definitely one fine man.

She noticed he'd scribbled his e-mail address on the bottom of his letter. Now the question was, how long would it take her to get up enough courage to write him?

December 22

A cold Seattle rain streamed down Kristin's bedroom window. Wind gusted against the eaves and rattled the barren alder branches outside. They moaned in protest, adding to the desolate feeling of the night.

But inside the house, she was warm and cozy. Snug in her favorite yellow flannel pajamas and thick slipper socks, she cuddled beneath her electric blanket and relaxed against the feather pillows piled up behind her. The laptop rested on the covers, the cursor patiently blinking.

It was now or never. She'd procrastinated long enough.

Okay, what should she say?

Her pair of Persians kept a wary eye on her, especially Minnie who did not approve of computers. The feline, curled on the foot of the bed, watched the glowing contraption with great displeasure. In her opinion, computers obviously did not belong on the bed.

Dear Ryan. Two o'clock. Saturday afternoon. I'm looking forward to it.

The phone startled her. Since she hadn't gotten online yet, she grabbed the cordless handset and glanced at the caller ID screen. "Hi, Mom."

"Hi. I know it's late, sweetie, but I wanted to check

in with you. You've been on my mind today. I've got all my shopping done except for you."

"I told you. Something for my house. Oh! Better yet, my kitchen."

"I can't think you'd like a mixer for Christmas. Lord knows when Pete bought me one for my birthday two years ago, I didn't take too kindly to it. It was sure a nice mixer, but Christmas is for something special."

"I know, but there's a lot of stuff I'd love to have."

"Well, I'll have to think about it. It doesn't seem right. Unless…" Excitement flickered across the miles. "You know a woman considering her future might want a well-stocked kitchen."

Oh, here it comes. Trust Mom to see buying a small appliance as a prelude to a trip down the aisle. "I agree, Mom. I should consider a future with a lot of small appliances in my kitchen. Since I'm a single career woman, I'm sure I'll enjoy healthier meals with my own, say, bread maker or one of those rotisserie roasters."

"Well, you just never know when you might be cooking for two."

"Exactly. Two weeks ago I went out to lunch with Cousin Rachel. It sure would have been nice to invite her over for a home-cooked meal."

"Oh, you! You know what I mean. I can't believe you want to be alone. Goodness. I'll rest so much better when I know you have a husband to take care of you in that big city you insist on living in."

"I like it here. I'm staying. Without a husband. Sorry."

"I worry. It's a dangerous world out there."

"I've got a security system."

"Well, I'll feel better knowing my last daughter is settled."

"I am settled, Mom. I have my own home, I have a great job, I'm happy. Why isn't that enough for you?"

"Oh, it is. But think of all that you're missing. A husband and children of your own. Kirby had a doctor's appointment—you know how they've had trouble trying for a second child—and I kept Michael so Sam could go with her to Bozeman for those tests she needs."

"I was just about to get online and check my messages. Kirby said she'd e-mail me if she felt up to it tonight and tell me what happened. How was Michael?"

"A handful! It took me back to when you girls were small. So much energy! It seemed as if I never could have a moment's rest, and now look at me. You're all grown and gone and I have all this time on my hands."

Kristin ached for her mom. For the child she'd had to bury, for the depression that troubled her for years after. Mom's life had crumbled into irrevocable pieces. It was sad, because Kristin had found a way to go on. She'd built a life that she could count on. Mom hadn't been as lucky.

"What's Dad up to now that he has so much time on his hands?"

"He's planted himself right in front of that expensive television he insisted on buying and doesn't move off the couch. Retirement is fine for him, but he's underfoot all day long."

Her parents had their problems. Kristin's stomach squeezed. Marriage. She didn't understand it. How her parents could have been so in love once—they'd been deeply bonded in the years when Kristin was small. But their marriage, as strong as it was, had suffered from their daughter's death. Now they were like two strangers living in the same house.

If love was something that could break, she didn't want any part of it, thank you very much!

"I had lunch with Mary again today. We had our own Christmas, just the two of us, a little early. We met at her house. I brought the eggnog and dessert, and she whipped up the best meal. Cornish game hens that were perfection. Anyway, she happened to mention that Ryan is coming home tomorrow. Isn't that something? He's finally got enough seniority in that doctor's office to get Friday and Saturday off. He'll be here, in Montana."

"I knew you were going to mention that. I already know, Mom."

"You do? You've spoken to him?"

"You sound as proud as if I'd won the Nobel Peace Prize. Mom!" Was her mother predictable or what? "He's not my type, and I'm not his. So stop. If you don't, I'm going to call each of my sisters and tell them that you're pressuring me. When you promised to stop."

"I just can't help myself. He's a *doctor*."

"Yeah. That's been established. Good night, Mom."

"Before you go, what time should I be looking for you tomorrow?"

"I'll be home sometime in the evening. Snow's forecasted through the mountain passes, so it'll be slow going. Don't wait supper on me."

"All right. You drive safe. I can't wait to see you. I love you, honey."

"I love you, too."

She hung up, aching. She loved her mother so much, but that only made Mom's comments about marriage hurt more. Mom's heart was in the right place, but she didn't understand. She couldn't. Her life was different. They were different women, different choices. That's what it came down to.

Wind moaned beneath the eaves, spattering rain against the windowpanes. The furnace kicked on, blowing at the closed curtains, ruffling them gently.

It was a lovely room. The big picture window, during the day, looked out over the grass lawn and through the treetops for a seasonal view of Green Lake. Gramma's old bedroom set, refinished in a honeyed oak, gleamed as if it were new. The reading chair tucked in the corner by the window, the oak bookcases stuffed with inspirational romances—this was home. Her home. Safe and snug and welcoming. Everything she'd ever wanted.

She'd never set her sights high on being rich or successful or renowned. She'd never wanted to base her future on unstable ground or on someone she could lose. But this place was nice and sensible at once, and it was her center. Her sanctuary. Her life. She was happy here. Content. Blessed.

The screen saver had clicked on and she tapped the keyboard to bring the e-mail program to the front. The letter sat, just as she'd left it.

She reread the e-mail, pondering. The mattress

dipped slightly as the second cat hopped onto the bed and padded across the quilt to inspect the screen. "What do you think, Mickey?"

The gray longhair sneered, lifted one paw and washed his face.

"You're right—I shouldn't meet him. It was a nice offer, to treat me to a milkshake. But with our match-making moms and all their hopes, it's a bad idea."

Ryan Sanders lived like two thousand miles away. Too far away to be friends. So what was the point? She didn't want another e-mail pen pal. She couldn't keep up with the messages she got from her sisters!

She hit Delete and clicked the command for the modem to start dialing. She read Kirby's letter first— a report on the state of her sister's fallopian tubes—and sent a sympathetic response. Then she moved on to Michelle's note about their joint gift for Mom. She laughed reading her last note from Kendra—who was getting her sleigh ready for the Christmas-tree expedition Christmas Eve morning.

She signed off without contacting Ryan.

Their lives had crossed paths once, for a higher purpose, perhaps only to save Samantha Fields. Kristin believed God worked that way, all things for His purpose and His good. That meant there was no reason she would see Ryan Sanders again. She wasn't about to manufacture one—not with the way her mom was frothing with excitement in hopes of a final marriage in the McKaslin family.

She tucked the computer onto the nightstand shelf,

eased into her feather pillows, soft and comfy, and switched off the lamp by her bed. In the dark, she drew the snuggly electric blanket to her chin.

Sure, she was alone, but she liked the peace of it. Rain hammered with a new fury on the roof above. Wind thrashed against the siding, making the fir boughs dance, their shadows from the faint porch light hovered on the wall.

This was her life—safe, predictable, independent, unshakable. She remembered to thank God for it before her heavy eyelids drifted shut and sleep claimed her.

December 23

Three minutes past midnight. Ryan yanked loose the tie that had been trying to throttle him for six hours. Way too long for a party, in his opinion. Their office Christmas party had taken place in one of Scottsdale's finest restaurants. The food had been amazing. The gifts generous. His heart hadn't been in the festivities. As usual.

He respected the people he worked with. He liked them as people. Talk about lucky. Not everyone could say that about the folks they worked with. He could make small talk, but he was beginning to think his former fiancée had been right. He was horrible when it came to getting really close to people.

He didn't want to get too close. That was the problem.

He tossed his tie on the bed. Francine had been right about a lot of things. He wasn't controlling, but he did control how much—or how little—he let people in.

He buried his emotions. He didn't express his feelings very well when he did allow them to surface. His career was demanding and left little time for any personal relationships. He pretty much kept to himself, other than the quick e-mail a few times a month, and superficial friendships with other busy doctors that were based mostly on talking about the job and sports.

Yeah, Francine was right on target.

The house echoed around him. Dark and shadowed. He rented it—it was easier than committing to a mortgage and taking on the added responsibility of being a homeowner. He'd worked hard to become a good surgeon. That took a great amount of devotion and responsibility.

Well, he wasn't a shrink. He didn't know a thing about psychology, not in the practical application. He only knew that for some reason the lonely shadows in his house felt as suffocating as the ones in his past. In his life.

He flicked on the hall light to chase away the darkness. That was enough introspection for one night. He was flying out tomorrow, that's why all this was troubling him.

Maybe he'd volunteer to work through the holidays next year. He loved his mom, but he couldn't take the memories. It had taken three weeks for him to stop waking up in the middle of the night in a sweat. The nightmares from his youth had returned. Dreams where he lost his mom, his sister, his home, everything that mattered. And his dad, over and over again.

He couldn't take going home, but he had to. How many times had he picked up the phone to dial his mom and cancel the trip? To try to explain to her? But how could he bring up his grief? Talking about Dad's death had always hurt her terribly. Over time she'd begun to mention him now and then in conversation, but to really talk, to go back in time—no, he couldn't do that to her.

He was going home tomorrow, whether he liked it or not.

In the bedroom he kicked off his shoes and shrugged out of his shirt. A paperback book was facedown, spine open on the crate he used as a bedside table. He usually read before he went to bed, but he didn't feel like it tonight.

What he needed to do was pack. He'd put it off, and since he had an early-morning flight, he'd run out of time. It was now or never.

The suitcase was buried on the floor of the closet where he'd left it after his last ski trip. He'd pack for cold weather. Maybe he'd be able to get some cross-country in while he was home. Mom wouldn't have any skis. Maybe he could borrow a pair somewhere, since there was no place in town that was likely to sell them. Kristin—he bet her family would have a few extra pairs of skis somewhere. Not that she'd taken him up on his offer of a milkshake.

She had a full life, too. She was probably busy, and it wasn't as if they had much in common.

It was just as well.

He tossed underwear, socks, jeans, a thin sweatshirt and a bunch of T-shirts. All warm-weather stuff, basically. He'd gotten rid of his winter clothes when he'd come here after his residency, and in the years that had followed, he'd bought only clothes suitable for Phoenix temperatures. As if, subconsciously, he was making a choice. In truth, he'd never intended to go home again.

He didn't want to go now.

He'd go to Montana this last time, but no more. Phoenix was home. This house was home. It was where his future was and where the past didn't crop up every time he looked out the window. The sparse brown and jagged rocks of the Southwest were as different from Montana as a man could get. He'd invite his mom and sister to visit him here instead for holiday gatherings.

He'd forgotten to pull the blinds, and as he grabbed his razor bag and headed for the bathroom, the flash of light caught his attention. The merry Christmas lights of the houses down the street—the Carlsons with the white icicle lights dangling from their tile roof, the Millers with multicolored bulbs cheerfully outlining their stucco home and the Cooks with their front yard saguaro cactus draped in solemn blue flashing lights.

There were no icicles dripping from his roofline. No lighted angels in his front window. No flashing strings of bulbs adorning the cactus in his front yard.

The shadows of the night felt cold. Hollow, he finished his packing and left the suitcase at the front door for easy grabbing on his way out the door at 5:00 a.m. He set his alarm, climbed in bed and left the tableside lamp on. The darkness felt as if it were closing in on him.

When sleep came, it was fitful. He could not find peace.

Chapter Eight

December 24

Kristin tugged her favorite cable-knit sweater over the white turtleneck she wore. The soft wool was deliciously warm. It would definitely keep her toasty on the sleigh ride into the hills. With a pair of long johns under her sturdiest pair of jeans and wool socks on her feet, she was ready for a McKaslin family tradition. Christmas-tree gathering, the same way her great-great-grandparents did when they homesteaded the ranch in the 1860s.

"Kristin! Hurry!" Mom's call echoed up the stairwell.

"I'm coming!" she answered just as there was a rattle at the back door. It was amazing she could hear it over the racket downstairs.

New greetings rose over the excited voices in the kitchen below. It sounded as if Mary was here.

Mary. Kristin froze in the hallway. If Mom had invited her best friend, then did that mean she'd invited Ryan, too?

No. There was no way a man like him would be interested in a sleigh ride into the hills. Relief sluiced through her. She couldn't imagine it—

"Merry Christmas, Mrs. McKaslin." A familiar male voice. *Ryan's* voice.

He was here. Her knuckles gripped the banister but she couldn't make her feet carry her forward. She hadn't answered his letter. Hadn't taken him up on his offer of a milkshake. And why? Because Mom would make such a big deal about it if she found out. Because she was under enough pressure. She'd disappointed her parents enough.

"Nice kitty." Allie, dainty and precious in her pink sweater that said Grandma's Little Princess and the cutest little pair of jeans, collapsed on the landing. Her arms wrapped around Minnie's middle and squeezed. "Soft kitty."

Kristin wasn't fooled by the disgruntled frown on the feline's face. She could hear the contented purr from six steps up. She stopped to give her three-year-old niece a kiss on the cheek.

"Kristin!" Mom sounded impatient. "We're leaving without you."

It was tempting, but she wasn't about to miss one of her favorite holiday customs. She'd have to talk to Mom about this later.

As for Ryan, she'd be polite to him. She liked him.

But she didn't *like* him. Mom would just have to accept that her and Mary's matchmaking was an abysmal failure.

As Kristin hurried to the kitchen, the merry ring of dozens of jingle bells filled the air with their sweet music. Two matched pairs of Clydesdales flashed past the dining-room window. In the next room, she could hear Mom ordering everyone outside and giving Karen last-minute instructions.

"I know, Mom, don't worry, just go," Karen said laughingly as she scooped up daughter number two and held the squiggling toddler captive on her hip. "Have a great time. Remember, I want something small. Not ten feet tall. Where's Dad? I'll tell him myself. Last Christmas you got us a tree that didn't fit in our house. Hi, Kris."

"Hey, big sister." Kristin gave Karen a hug and baby Anna a raspberry kiss that made the toddler giggle. "Yeah, where's Dad?"

"He headed into town to have breakfast." Mom's words were tight, but her smile was firmly in place.

Her fake smile. The one she used when she didn't want to acknowledge something was wrong.

Kristin saw the question on Karen's face, too. Dad leaving for town on a day like this? Getting the family Christmas trees was something he looked forward to every year. Kristin opened her mouth to ask if they should wait, but Karen shook her head.

That could only mean one thing—there had been serious discord between Mom and Dad. Perhaps they'd had an argument or a heated fight. Maybe this was the one that would tear them apart for good.

Kristin's stomach twisted. *Please, Lord. Not now.* Since the birth of their first grandchild, her parents had been on speaking terms and had been creeping incrementally closer to one another. And now, who knew? She just wanted them to love each other the way they used to.

"I'll join Mary outside. Kristin, you'll close the door behind you?" Mom handed her a thick parka and a pair of gloves. She looked frail and tired.

Why hadn't she noticed that last night when she'd arrived? Because she'd been tired herself after about fifteen hours on the road. She was still tired.

"Sure." She waited until Mom was out of hearing range to whisper to Karen. "What about their gift?"

"Yeah. I know." Karen looked troubled, too, as she set Anna down on her pink tennis shoes. The toddler took off on a flat-footed gait after Mickey, who was hiding beneath the table. "Pray."

"Yeah. Big-time."

Snow drifted on the wind, tiny spun-sugar flakes, as delicate as air. They caught on her lashes and tickled her cheek as she zipped up her old winter coat. She tugged the back door shut behind her, lost. What were they going to do about their parents?

"I say we don't fight it." A man's melted-butter baritone had her turning around. Ryan, chainsaw in hand, waded through the knee-deep snow from the direction of the detached garage.

"Fight what? And why do you have Dad's chain saw? Oh, I get it. That's what you're doing here."

"Yep. Believe me, I'm freezing and it's early and I'd rather be reading the morning paper in front of the woodstove. But my mom and yours pleaded with me. Since Pete isn't going to work the chain saw, they needed a man, they said. I couldn't turn them down."

"Our moms have way too much time on their hands. I know how to work a chain saw. I helped Dad every year bring in wood for the winter. So did Karen and Kendra."

"So basically I'm here under false pretenses?" Ryan watched her nod and it didn't surprise him—not one bit. Yeah, Mom was up to no good. Just as he'd suspected. "Our moms have worked so hard plotting how to put us together. Like I said, why fight it? It will only make them try harder."

"I'm sorry about this." Fiery pink crept across Kristin's fine-boned face.

Ryan doubted it was from the cold wind alone. He understood, and he hated seeing the reserved way she was keeping distance between them. Normally that kind of thing didn't bother him, but he liked Kristin. She was into her career, that was her focus. He sure understood that, and he figured they had to stick together against the marriage-minded. "Don't be sorry. We'll ignore them. What's the saying around these parts—you can lead a horse to water but you can't make him drink?"

"You can't make *her* drink," she corrected, and some of that fiery sparkle returned to her eyes.

Yeah, she was a girl with spunk. Ryan held out his hand. "Let's make them pay for manipulating us. C'mon, friend."

He loved her smile. Big, bold, genuine. When she smiled, it was like sunshine on a snow that lit up the entire world.

She slid her delicate hand into his. "You're on, friend. Do you know how to use that chain saw?"

"How can you ask that? I'm a Montana boy at heart."

"Yeah, but you're a city man now."

"No more than you're an urban woman. Cutting down a tree is something every real man knows. My dad used to take me up into the woods when I was a kid. Don't worry. I know how to use this thing." He hiked the dangling chain saw for emphasis.

Kristin bit her bottom lip to keep quiet. Testosterone!

"Hurry up, you two!" Kendra popped up beside the giant horses, tugged on the harness, patted one of the gentle giants on the neck and took up the reins. "Ryan, have you ever been on a horse-drawn sleigh?"

"No, ma'am. Looks like I'm in for a treat. Aren't the little ones coming along?"

"It's too dangerous," Kristin answered, stole the chain saw from him and stowed it safely beneath the front board seat. She talked to her sister in a low whisper, heads together, in the way that women do, before leaving Kendra to settle the dual set of thick leather reins between her gloved fingers. "Karen's staying behind with the kids. Allie might be old enough next year."

That made sense. The chilly temperature alone was enough to give a guy hypothermia. Of course, maybe that had more to do with the thin summer-weight sweatshirt he had on beneath Dad's old coat. The goose-down parka cut a lot of the wind's bite, but not enough. And it only covered him so much. His legs and feet were bone cold.

His mom had taken up position on the board seat next to Kendra, and she looked proud of herself. "You two find a place and sit down."

"Sure, Mom." Yeah, he was going to have to have a talk with her. Set it out straight and tell her how it was. And not just about Kristin. About Dad, coming here— *everything*. But now wasn't the time.

Kristin climbed aboard the sleigh, which was more of a sled for hauling than riding. A layer of local hay, sweet smelling and soft, lined the back in a fluffy bed. She snuggled in, sitting so her feet dangled off the back.

He climbed in beside her. "So, you people do this every year?"

"Sure. It never occurred to me that other people didn't cut their own trees every year, until I was away at college and saw a Christmas-tree lot. I laughed so hard, I cried."

"There aren't a lot of fir trees in Phoenix. They have to truck them in. It costs a bundle for a real tree. So I bought a plastic one. It stays in a box for pretty much a whole year and I let Mom take it out when she comes down."

"Plastic trees. Yeah, that's what I put up in my house.

I have one of those little ones. My cats hate it, but it's simpler, since I always come here for Christmas."

"Yeah." Christmas. Ryan hated to think about the lights he didn't put up and the tree still in its box in the garage. "It doesn't seem right without my dad."

He heard the words coming out of his mouth. Too honest. Too private. He stared down at the coat he wore, the navy-blue nylon flecked with snowflakes, and willed the pain to stay down. Didn't quite succeed at it.

The sleigh jerked forward, the skids squeaking on the fresh snow. Ryan's bones rattled. His teeth clacked together. His spine snapped. The jarring start smoothed out into a sensation of gliding. The tiny bells on the harnesses made a sweet sound. "Not too bad."

"Wait until the horses pick up speed. Then it's like flying. Oh! Here we go! Hold on!" Her gloved hands curled around the ends of the floorboards as the sleigh pitched again, accentuated by the jingling bells, and eased into an eye-watering cruising speed.

It was too cold to talk, with the wind whipping by. Silence was the best way to enjoy the ride as she got caught up in the rhythmic chink of the horses' hooves on the compacted snow, the caroling bells and the lilting rhythm of the women's voices in the seat up front. Somehow, Ryan's melancholy seemed out of sync with the pleasant grassy scent of the hay, and the snowflakes falling in a lazy waltz from a white-gray sky that went on forever.

Despite his soul-deep pain, Ryan savored the sheer exhilaration of the snow-mantled earth flying out from under him, the solemn stance of wooden fence posts wearing snowlike hats, their wooden rails outstretched like arms. Nothing moved, not bird or deer or rabbit except for the crystal flakes everywhere descending.

Kristin leaned close, bringing with her the scent of fabric softener and vanilla. Her scarf felt like a kitten's fur against his cheek. Something sharp as a pin's prick jabbed him deep inside, turning him inward again. His chest ached and he felt...

He didn't know what he felt.

The earth felt solemn, as if sleeping. The morning was calm as the valley fields rolled away and the horses started to climb. Random trees appeared, then more and more, until it was a forest draped in white, silent with grace. It felt as if something were speaking to him, not with words, but to his heart. A tug that pulled at his very sturdy defenses.

He watched her as she breathed deep the cold air and lifted her face to the sky.

"This ride blows me away every year." She blinked at the snowflakes caught on her eyelashes. "I've done nothing for the last three weeks but shop and stress and worry and rush here and there. Wait through traffic without moving. Circle parking garages for over half an hour looking for any old spot to park in. Push my way through crowded malls and wait in long lines. On top of work, feeling like there's never enough time and so much to do."

"I did all my shopping late. Made a list, made one stop at the mall. Caught a bunch of sales, wasn't too bad at all. Okay, I only have Mom and Mia to buy for, except for the office girls at work and my nurse, so it's not bad. We don't have a big family, the way you do."

"Yeah. But when I'm here, feeling the snow on my face and seeing it grace the trees, it hits me every time. All the stress melts away. Nothing has changed, not in two thousand years. All the hustle and hurry-up and decorating and gift buying is all done because of a single child born long ago. That the heart of Christmas is the same and always will be."

"I hear it wasn't easy for the Wise Men, either. Sure, they didn't have mall traffic to deal with, but they rode forever on a camel's back. Think of it. No air-conditioning. No roadside convenience stores. No motels or fast food along the way. No Global Positioning System. No triple A."

"I hadn't quite thought of it like that before." When she laughed, the sound was as dulcet as the bells ringing.

Whatever was hurting within him lifted through him like a bird in flight, filling his eyes so he turned away. It was the cold making his eyes tear.

Nothing more.

The sleigh slowed to a stop on snow so pure, it looked like clouds. The sun poked out between a break in the clouds to smile on the wintry forest, and a billion glimmers shone everywhere making the world so bright, it hurt to look at it.

"Notice how they sent us out to scout for trees." Ryan's stride was bigger than hers, and the knee-deep snow hardly troubled him.

"I noticed." Kristin trekked beside him, working harder to keep up with him. The snow was deep and dangerous. While they weren't in the mountains, snow pack avalanching off the ridge nearby had them sticking to the thicker woods, where the trees offered protection.

Though it made it tougher to hike. She pushed aside a branch, and snow cascaded down on her, slipping between her collar and the back of her neck. Talk about freezing. She shivered. "I don't know if they're trying to pair us up or give us hypothermia."

"Yeah, notice how they didn't offer us one of those thermoses your sister brought with her. Hot chocolate?"

"And coffee." Kristin knew from experience. "When we were kids, Mom would bundle all of us up and Granddad would come by on his sled. Gramma was the one who brought the hot drinks then, and a bag of homemade Christmas cookies, too, and we'd sing carols all the way up and all the way back. But things change."

"People leave you."

"Yep. First Granddad. Then Allison. You said it doesn't seem right without your dad. That's the way it is with me, too. I don't know how my sisters do it. They go on, they get married, have kids. I don't know. I guess they've coped with it in their own ways, but I can't pretend Allison didn't die. It's like saying she didn't exist, that she didn't matter."

"Yeah." Ryan sounded choked. "Yeah."

Because it hurt, she said nothing more. Let the cold chap her face and burn down her throat when she breathed. "What about that one?"

"I think it would be just the right size for Mom's living room. Here, let me get this contraption started." Pointing the tip downward, safely away from their feet, he yanked on the starter. The small motor coughed before it started on the second pull. The earsplitting whine shattered the serenity.

Kristin held the shoulder-high cedar by the trunk, as Ryan knelt to dig the saw into the bark at the snow line. The vibration rocketed through her arm until the tree came loose. The roar died, and Ryan set the saw aside as she kept the young tree from falling on its perfect branches.

Yep, he was a Montana boy at heart, just as he'd said. He handled the chain saw with the same competence that he did everything.

When he helped her lay the tree gently on its side in the snow, the solid length of his arm bumped hers. He was one hundred percent substantial man. Dependable. Amazing.

Was it her imagination, or was her pulse skyrocketing?

He hiked the chain saw up by the handle. Snow clung to him everywhere—hair, jaw, shoulders and thighs. "Your family wouldn't happen to have an extra pair of cross-country skis, would they?"

It took a few seconds for her brain to register his

question. "Uh, in the garage. I'll check when we get back."

"Thanks. I appreciate it. Mom sold my old pair at a garage sale, like ten years ago." He trudged toward a huddle of firs. "These trees are about eight feet. Think your sisters would like them?"

Kristin squinted at the threesome of evergreens. It was easy to imagine each proudly bearing twinkle lights on their tender branches.

By the time they'd cut all three trees, she and Ryan were working together as a team. She held the tree, he used the saw, and they stacked the trees carefully to keep the limbs and needles from being damaged.

"Can I ask you something pretty personal?" Beneath the arching pines and reaching cedar, he looked more dream than man as the sunlight faded, leaving him in shadow.

She felt rooted in place as snow began to pummel down, tapping on her coat, catching in her hair. It was as if a veil shrouded them, and although their mothers and Kendra were just on the other side of the rise, maybe ten yards away, the curtain closed around just the two of them.

It felt as if they were the only two people anywhere.

Did Ryan feel this, too? She swallowed. "What do you want to know?"

He leaned so close all that separated them was the snow-filled air. "You lost your sister years ago. How can you do it? Come back here and go on. How did you make everything okay?"

"It's not. It will never be fine again."

"Then how can you come home year after year? How do you get past it? I—" Pain lined his face, shadowed his eyes, tensed his jaw.

He was talking about his father. Sympathy tugged in her chest and she reached out. His arm was iron solid beneath her fingertips. The image of him that night when he'd helped the car-accident victim arrowed into her mind. He'd been awesome. She'd never have guessed he had wounds of his own that would never heal.

She knew exactly what that felt like. "I—"

"Ryan? Kristin?" Mom's voice carried on the rising wind. "Where did you two get off to?"

Kristin withdrew her hand as her mother trudged into sight, but it was too late. Mom was already grinning from earmuff to earmuff. "Interrupted you, I see. Ryan, be a dear and come with me. We've found the perfect tree for my living room."

Mary joined them, and there was Kendra leading the double team of horses. Kristin stayed behind, insisting on helping load the trees, while Ryan stepped through the mist and disappeared. She and Kendra loaded the cut trees with care, while Mary broke out the thermoses.

Although Ryan was no longer beside her, Kristin could feel the echoes of his pain. Of his grief. Or maybe it was simply her own.

Mary talked of her daughter Mia who was expected home today, and of the candlelight service at the church tonight. Hopefully the storm wouldn't make the roads treacherous.

When Ryan returned, breaking through the curtain of snowfall with the tree hefted on his wide shoulder, she looked away. Willing her pulse to slow to normal, she quieted the beat of sympathy for him in her heart.

She didn't want to talk about the past or her family's loss. The storm blew hard from the north, the arctic winds chasing them down the hillside and through the fields to the ranch house on McKaslin land.

She couldn't endure the hope on her mom's face as she watched them so carefully for the tiniest signal that a romance was about to blossom between them. Ryan seemed quiet and he didn't meet her gaze as he unloaded the tree meant for the living room. He carried it inside, and she took the chance to dash to the garage. Finding an old pair of Dad's skis, which he never used anymore, she secured them on the sleigh.

By the time Ryan stepped out of the house, she was heading back to the garage for the big storage bins of ornaments. He drove off in the sleigh alone on the bed, his big feet dangling off the back as the whiteout conditions stole him away.

While she untangled tree lights, hung delicate glass balls, or even when she'd plugged in the star atop the tree, he never left her thoughts.

Nor did the ache within her. It felt as if he'd put another one there, deep into her heart where she could take no more. As Bing Crosby sang of a white Christmas, the daylight waned. The blizzard struck hard against the northwest walls of the house, cutting off the outside world. She wondered if he was thinking of her.

"Oh, now it feels like Christmas." Mary Sanders stepped back to study her workmanship. The multicolored lights twinkled on boughs of evergreen. Little toy soldiers and jolly Santas and heavenly angels hung from the tips of every branch. At the top, the same angel his father had bought the year before he died glowed with a bright assurance.

Christmas has never been the same without you, Dad. Ryan rested his face in his hands. The feelings rising within him were too much. He tried to shut down, but couldn't. They were too powerful. A train of images chugging through his brain. Dad, young and tall and alive, kneeling down before a Christmas tree in the same corner of the same living room, his voice a low baritone and warm with affection. "Let's see what else Santa brought. Here's a present for you, Ryan. And look, Mia, this one's for you." His little sister, preschool age with brown ringlet curls, took the package with her eager hands.

Another Christmas. Another image. Of Dad seated on the floor beside him, the fire roaring in the stone fireplace, puzzling out the deluxe train set Santa had brought. So much track, so many crossings and bridges. By the time Mom had the Christmas ham out of the oven for the noon meal, a train tooted as it raced on the track lapping the living room and winding around the huge dollhouse, where Mia was busily setting up furniture.

The last Christmas with Dad. He'd been laid off, and they'd done without a lot of gifts, but Santa had come through. Ryan hadn't thought of it at the time, but he realized now how tight his father had to scrimp and save, and how much he'd had to sacrifice to make sure there were gifts beneath the tree. Ryan had been speechless with joy when he saw his dream gift—a sleek black bike with the knobby tires and shiny chrome. And his elation intensified listening to Mia squeal with delight over the array of Barbie stuff she'd gotten.

That was the year he'd learned there was no Santa Claus. When he'd asked Dad, his father had said gently, "There is if you believe."

He'd always resented that his dad had lied about it. He knew there was no jolly man in a red suit that came down the chimney. Dad had died a month later and taken the last of Ryan's illusions.

"Tired?" Mom ruffled his hair, running her fingers round the cowlick in the center of his head as she'd done all his life.

Tired? Hardly. His soul felt weary.

"Here, have a candy cane." She held out a red-and-green-and-white-striped candy. "Spearmint. Your favorite."

"Thanks." He took the treat and tore off the wrapper while his mom sat down beside him.

"I don't see you in my living room nearly often enough." Mom sounded serious, the way she did when she was about to give one of her wise-mother lectures.

He didn't think he could take it. Everywhere he

looked were memories of Dad. Wearing his coat today had been too much. He felt as if he were ready to explode like a keg of old dynamite. "Don't start, Mom. You know I have a hard time around the holidays."

"I know you were close to your father. So was I, you know." Her love was patient and warm, like a candle glowing in the dark, like hope in the midst of despair.

Lord knew how she'd been that light for him, as a boy, broken to the soul over his dad's death. He'd been too young to understand it well. Only that his father was gone. That there would be no more early-morning treks into the marshes, no more tracking the white-tailed deer.

No more magic winter mornings as calm as heaven's grace.

No more family.

They'd scrambled and fought to survive for so long, to keep hold of the house and food on the table, that there had been no time for grief.

He'd lived his adult life the same way. Little time for play, less time for living. He remained, deep inside, that same little boy trying to survive. To do his best to help provide for his mom and sister. Even now after the crisis had long passed.

"Your father watches over us, I know he does." Mom rubbed away the tears from her eyes. "Heaven knows if anyone deserves to be an angel, it was that man. The best husband a woman could ask for."

"The best dad."

"I know this stubbornness of yours, of not finding a nice girl and settling down—"

"No, please." Pain clawed through his chest with sharp talons, leaving him ragged and bleeding. "I tried that. I wasn't any good at it. Francine wasn't at fault. She was a great person. I just—" *Can't get close to anyone.*

He couldn't let his mom any closer, either. Panic had him launching out of the recliner and across the room. The tree lights blinked in a merry rhythm, sending enough light to guide him through the dark room and into the kitchen. Where a plate of Mia's favorite iced Christmas cookies waited, a treat for when she finally arrived.

"Ryan." Mom followed him. Love was in her voice—and concern. "Where are you going?"

"Mia's here." At least he figured the twin beams slicing through the whiteout were his sister's. She was home safe, finally, and Mom could devote all her motherly energies to Mia. Good. Because he was going out.

He grabbed the coat and elbowed open the door. Bitter wind needled through him as he struggled into the parka. He didn't care about the worsening storm or the dangerous temperatures. As Mia's old Toyota skidded to a stop in the driveway, he knocked on the back-quarter panel.

The trunk lid popped with a tired groan. He grabbed the heavy suitcases and book bag and hauled them into the back door. He ignored his mom's distress over him and kissed her on the cheek.

"Take care of Mia," he said as he grabbed gloves

from the hooks over the furnace register. "She's had a long hard drive. I'll be fine."

He steeled his heart against the sadness on Mom's face and the confusion on his sister's as he strode away into the snowy night.

Chapter Nine

"What are we gonna do about Mom and Dad's present?" Michelle whispered when Dad disappeared into the kitchen to answer the knock at the back door. "Karen, Kirby and Kendra kept calling me, like I'm supposed to know. I've got, like, no clue what to do."

"Me, either."

Kristin managed to breathe around the knot in her throat. The one that came from watching her parents all evening. How they ignored each other. How they spoke to one another, when at all, tersely. How much distance they kept—Mom in the kitchen or in her chair by the fire, Dad on the couch. Finally Mom had retired upstairs to read in bed, and hadn't bothered to glance in her husband's direction as she left the room.

"Tell me again why you got married?" Kristin asked her baby sister.

"I was forced at gunpoint." Pretending to be totally serious, Michelle stole another macaroon from the plate of cookies on the coffee table in front of her. "Hmm. I love these and, lucky for me, I'm eating for two." She smiled. It was not a superficial grin, but one that came from deep within.

True happiness. Okay, so her sisters were happy with their lives and marriages. Fine. She understood that. But what about down the road? Romantic love didn't last. It was a bright fire that quickly burned out, and then, from what she could see, there was only darkness and ashes. Silences that felt razor sharp.

No, she wanted a life built on a more solid foundation than that.

"I hear you and Ryan are getting pretty tight." Michelle waggled her eyebrows. "It was all Mom could talk about on the way to church."

"And on the way back." Kristin leaned forward on the couch, studied the colorful choices on the cookie plate and chose a red-sprinkled Santa. "What happened between Mom and Dad? I thought they were doing better."

In the kitchen, Dad's voice rose in greeting, his words indistinguishable over the noise of the TV.

"I don't know. They were doing better. Having grandchildren was starting to really bring them together, or so I *thought*. Anyway, who knows? Dad is closed up tight. And Mom refuses to talk about it. Believe me, I tried. *You* should go talk to her."

"Okay."

"Good. That's probably my husband. I'm going to take my daughter and another one of these—" She stole a macaroon from the plate. "I'm outta here. Merry

Christmas. We'll be over after Emily unwraps all her loot from Santa."

"Merry Christmas."

Michelle lifted Emily's carrier from the floor, where she slept peaceful and warm in her pink flannel sleeper. Her golden curls were mussed, corkscrewing around her cherub's face, making her look angelic.

Brody poked his head around the corner to wish her a Merry Christmas and to take his sleeping daughter from his wife. His strong arm wrapped around Michelle's slim shoulders, drawing her close, and they walked away together into the brightness of the kitchen and out of sight, blessed by the halo of twinkle lights spanning the arched doorway.

They looked like a team. Like a unit. Together and happy.

But hadn't Mom and Dad been the same way once?

Voices rose from the kitchen—probably Karen's husband, Zach, come by to fetch the present Mom and Dad had been hiding for them. Not in the mood for network television, Kristin grabbed the remote and clicked off the power.

Silence settled into the room like the snow outside. The white lights on the fragrant fir tree glowed pure and true. The glass balls reflecting a thousand pinpricks of light. The star topping the tree shone in memory of the star burning brightly centuries ago on this very night.

Minnie hopped soundlessly onto the cushion and curled into a ball on Kristin's lap. She threaded her fingers through the cat's silky fur and was rewarded with a contented purr.

How can you come home year after year? How do you get past it? Ryan's question troubled her in the quiet moments. She'd been able to put it aside as she and Mom decorated the tree and then hurried to put supper on the table on time. Michelle and Brody had joined them, with little Emily, who kept them entertained as she banged in rhythm on her high-chair tray to the Christmas songs Michelle had been teaching her.

It had been a busy night. First, there were the dishes, and a quick change of clothes and the journey to church in the near blizzard conditions. Then, the service and the traditional gathering of the entire clan, cousins and all, at the cousin's restaurant. And finally, dessert, gift exchange and then the drive home.

She'd hardly had a moment to herself, but now that she did, Ryan's question troubled her. She missed her sister. She missed the family she used to have. The closeness. The happiness. Was that why her sisters had all married? In the attempt to find that time again?

And if so, then how long would it last? Didn't they know you couldn't trust someone else to build your life around? That standing on your own two feet was the best bet?

"Wow. You look deep in thought." A man's broad silhouette ambled from the bright kitchen. Ryan. "I'm interrupting."

"No. Come in. Have a cookie. I didn't hear you drive up."

"That's because I skied."

"You know there's a blizzard out there, right? They closed down, like, half the county roads."

"I *am* a little cold. Oh good, a fire." He crouched down in front of the hearth—all six feet plus of him. Orange light danced across him and he held out his hands. "Wow, that feels good. I saw you with your family at church tonight. I tried to catch up to you, but there were too many people."

Kristin gently scooted Minnie into the crook of her arm and made her way over. She snagged the cookie plate as she passed by. "I didn't see you or your mom."

"We came late. Sat in the back. We didn't want to leave home until we heard from Mia."

"Was she driving home from school?"

"Oh, I love these." He grabbed a gingerbread man decorated in colorful icing. After his first bite, he moaned. "Anyway, yeah, she's home safe and sound. I was pretty worried about her."

"Sisters are pretty precious."

"That they are."

And here she was trying not to think about Allison. She slid the plate on the corner of the hearth. "You've got to be freezing. I can feel the cold radiate off you."

"Yeah, I stopped feeling my toes halfway here."

"And why didn't you turn around and head home?"

"It's complicated. I guess I just needed a friend."

"Then you're in luck. First, we'd better warm you up. We have tea, coffee or cocoa."

"You said the magic word. Do you have marshmallows?"

"What's cocoa without them? Just a cup of chocolate. Sit down." She curved around the hearth, laid the cat on the nearby recliner and swept from the room, leaving him alone in the shadows.

But not in the dark. White twinkle lights draped from the window valences to circle the room. Bigger bulbs decorated the ten-foot fir that he'd cut for Mrs. McKaslin. Elegance was the word he'd use to describe the tree. Fragile white glass balls and handblown glass angels.

When he got up to take a closer look, he realized there were words etched into the glass. "In memory of our own angel, Allison, Christmas 2000." Another bore the current year. Another nearly eight years in the past. Mrs. McKaslin must have hired a local artist to make an ornament every year for a daughter she still loved.

Yeah, that was the problem, wasn't it? Love died with the loved one, and then where did that leave you? Cold through to his soul, he retreated to the fire where it seemed the heat couldn't touch him. Where the light couldn't find him.

Kristin returned. She set a tray on the coffee table, kneeling to unload it. Two steaming oversize mugs. Spoons. A plastic bag of marshmallows. Her movements caught his eye. A Polaroid picture was propped against a crystal candlestick holder.

He leaned closer to get a good look. A preschool blond-haired little girl with the bluest eyes. McKaslin eyes. She was dressed in red velvet and white lace. Her baby sister—a year-old identical replica—stood beside her, ringlet curls bobbing. Next to them, frozen in the act of stomping his foot hard on the floor, was a dark-haired boy.

Two other smaller girls completed the photograph. Michelle's year-old daughter, who looked exactly like her mama. And a small infant lay cradled in a car seat carrier—the newest addition to the family. A new generation of McKaslins.

"Little Caitlin. She belongs to Kendra and Cameron, but I stole her as much as I could today."

"A little fond of your sisters' kids?"

"You could say that. They're all so precious." Kristin sank to the floor beside him, the soft fuzz of her sweater's sleeve an intimate brush against his wrist as she leaned in to study the picture.

A gold cross on a chain fell out from the neckline of her sweater and swayed back and forth, drawing his gaze. He admired her heart-shaped face, the firelight in her hair, the delicate cut of her neck, shoulders and arms.

Vanilla tickled his nose and a roar filled his ears. A strange, bittersweet yearning broke through the ice around his heart and punched him. Left him without breath. Awareness zinged through him, surging through nerves and veins, warming him from his chest outward. What was wrong with him? Maybe he was more hypothermic than he thought.

Kristin scooted the plastic bag across the table. "Add

more marshmallows. You don't have enough melted fluff in that cocoa. True cocoa enjoyment is all about proportion. Tons of chocolate. Tons of melty marshmallows. There are scientific studies proving the healing benefits of it."

"I think I read one just last week in one of my medical journals."

"See? Cocoa makes everything better." Kristin swirled the spoon through her brimming mug, mixing melted fluff with the rich milky chocolate.

It was his senses mixing, too. He couldn't tear his attention away from the dazzling highlights glinting in her hair, shining a hundred different shades of gold in the glow of the fireplace and the faint shine of the lights from the Christmas tree behind her.

It had been a bitter-cold journey through the dark, that was all, that was why he was feeling this way. The warm room, the steaming cocoa and Kristin's brightness combined against the cold that ached in his bone marrow had him hurting.

A mild case of frostbite. His blood was warming his extremities, that explained his physiological symptoms. He'd be lucky if he didn't come down with pneumonia. He wasn't a greenhorn; he was a Montanan, born and bred. But it had been oblivion he'd been seeking when he ran out into the storm. The cold had frozen him down to the soul.

He'd skied with all his might, skidding down gullies and kicking up hills by memory. The years he'd been away had seemed to fall away, and he'd known where the fences were that separated fields and marked property lines. He'd known the deep irrigation ditch siding the country road he'd used for the last quarter-mile stretch. He'd found his way, succeeding in losing his pain.

For a while.

But he was thawing. So was his pain, which coursed through him like the blood in his veins. His fingertips seared and throbbed. Nothing serious, so he ignored it and wrapped his hands around the big stoneware mug with hollyberries rimming a Christmas scene.

He'd been wrong to come here. He'd tried to get away from the holiday memories in his mom's house, but this was no better.

Did the McKaslins know how to do anything halfway? Christmas was everywhere, from the ten-foot tree decorated like an interior designer had gotten hold of it, piled with gifts beneath, to the wreaths on the walls. Twinkle bulbs raced along the ceiling and cast light like stardust onto a snowy Christmas village on the mantel. Peppermint-striped candles sat in snowflake-shaped holders, and the scents of pine and wood smoke grabbed him by the throat and squeezed.

Voices rose from the kitchen. Gruff male voices followed by the *clink* of metal hitting the floor. Before the past could jerk him backward in time, the fire popped like a gunshot and Kristin leaped up to sweep the burning spark off the carpet and onto the stone hearth. The ember glowed brightly, pulsing with light and dark.

With the present and the past. Ryan realized he'd

been holding the cup in midair, so he took a big gulp. Chocolaty and sweetly frothy, it burned him from his tongue to his stomach lining.

Kristin settled back to her spot on the floor, cringing from the sounds from the kitchen. Dad had offered to help Zach put Allie's new tricycle together. Judging by the sound of things, there were a few problems.

A horrible clash of metal reverberated through the house followed by the angry sounds of displeasure coming from her dad. She heard Zach's frustrated comment on the inadequacy of the directions and a missing screw. There was a bang of the back door, the eerie howl of the wind.

Dad was probably going to search through the garage to see if he had something in his toolbox that would work. She hoped he bundled up first. She took her mug with her as she crossed to the window. There was nothing—only night reflected back to her in the shine of the glass and the glow from the tree lights. Ice clung in filmy streaks along the edges of the panes.

"The storm's getting worse." Ryan spoke behind her. He'd come without a sound. The light from the tree and the fire lapped around him, stroking the long neat lines of him, of his breadth, his height. A substantial man, even in shadow. "Maybe I'd better get home before—"

The wind punched the house with a fury that rattled the windows. That seemed to move the entire structure an inch off the foundation. Black pellets scoured the glass and the sudden chill penetrating the window had her shivering.

"Maybe I won't be heading home just yet." Ryan's hand settled on her shoulder.

Comfort. That's what his touch gave her. Not a friendly kind of comfort, or a brotherly kind of steadiness. The weight of his palm on the curve of her neck, the heat of him, the might. He felt powerful enough to protect her from the wind and darkness, the cold and the night. Her entire being sparkled in the silence that seemed to fall between them.

There was only him, the sound of his breathing, the rustle of his socks on the carpet as he shifted his weight to draw her away from the cold. The winter-and-man scent of him and the faint hint of fabric softener on his shirt. The shadows in her heart seemed to fade, and the ache vanished.

Dad, raking snow out of his hair, stepped into the archway. The wind was too loud to have heard him come in, but there he was, safe and sound, his dear face chapped red from his trek outside. "Ryan, you'd best stay here for a bit. And whatever you do, don't go skiing back. I'll leave my keys on the counter. You take my truck, you hear? It's four-wheel drive. It'll get you home safe."

"Thanks, Mr. McKaslin. I appreciate it."

"You wouldn't happen to know anything about tricycles, would ya? I've worked on farm machinery all my life, and Zach's a mechanic. You'd think between the two of us, we could put a kid's trike together." Dad shook his head, managing a smile.

But he looked weary. And old. Her daddy was looking old.

When had that happened? Kristin went to him, feeling as fragile as glass. Although they rarely spoke of it, this time of year was hardest on him, too. "You look like you need a cup of cocoa and some help. You're in luck."

"I've been known to be handy with a wrench, in a pinch." Ryan's deep voice vibrated through her, and it felt as if for an instant they were connected.

Maybe it just felt that way because they were united in purpose. Kristin made cocoa and gave her opinion on various interpretations of the instructions while the men worked. Dad, with tension etched deep into his face. Zach, frustrated and checking the time as the evening vanished. Ryan looking less troubled with something to keep him busy.

Yet she could still feel his sadness as if it were her own.

There had been something calming about the frustration over the construction of the tricycle. Ryan rubbed at the tension in his neck from leaning and twisting trying to get the handlebars in place. It had taken a mechanic, a farmer and a surgeon nearly forty minutes to reach success. Zach had left with a perfect pink-and-white trike covered with a tarp in the back of his truck.

"Well, good night to you, young man." Mr. McKaslin set empty mugs on the counter, lost in shadows. "I'm goin' on up to bed. Don't you forget to take my truck."

"Thanks, sir." The winds were dying, the blizzard beginning to wind down. He needed to get back, it was nearly midnight. Since the phone lines were dead and his cell wasn't picking up a signal, his mom was likely to be worried about him.

Celebration marked this room, too. The kitchen and eating area were huge and homey. Multicolor twinkle lights flashed in a cheerful rhythm from the archways and the tops of cabinets, threading over plant shelves and draping from valences. A ceramic nativity scene waited patiently on the polished wood of the window seat. Why the sight of the porcelain mother and child made Ryan's chest hurt, he didn't know. Too many feelings, too much regret? Probably.

There was something about this house, too. This home with its feeling of family in the very air. Of closeness. He could sense what tomorrow would be like. Of the women laughing and working and filling up the kitchen, preparing the Christmas meal. The little kids underfoot, with new toys and limitless energy and munching on those great Christmas cookies. The shouts of the men in the living room and the sound of a game would fill the house.

He remembered on Thanksgiving how it was. A family come together to celebrate.

His chest felt wide open. He'd been wrong to come. Wrong to stay. Foolish to think that he could escape by coming here. Blindly, he grabbed his dad's old coat from the back of the kitchen chair, where it had been drying. He'd come here for a reason.

He unzipped the side pocket, where a small thin box was buried. It had been there all day. He'd grabbed it when Kendra had been by to pick him and Mom up in her sleigh, and he'd totally forgotten. And by the looks of it, it had survived.

It wasn't the only thing in his pocket.

Ryan set aside the box. His heart began to pound in double rhythm. His fingers fumbled as he withdrew the envelope. Ryan was written in a man's hand— Dad's handwriting—on the front.

Why hadn't he noticed this before? Hands shaking, knees weak, he sank into the nearest chair. His fingers working the card loose from the envelope without thought. In the glow of the twinkle lights, he saw it was a card meant for a kid. There was a cartoon dog on the front and big block letters proclaiming, Happy Birthday to the Best Son Ever!

Oh, God. Why hadn't anyone found this? Ryan put it down. Picked it back up. It looked as though there was handwriting inside the card—more of Dad's handwriting.

He squeezed his eyes shut, holding his breath. Freezing every emotion inside him before he broke apart. Before the little boy inside him could remember.

He concentrated on the faint clink and clunk from the next room. The rush and rustle wrapping paper made when it was unrolled. The snap of Scotch tape. The squeak of a bow as it was stretched and twisted. Kristin must be wrapping last-minute gifts. He could hear her gentle frustration, "Mickey! I don't need any help, thank you very much!"

The ripple of her chuckle was warm and wonderful. Soft as silver it seemed to hook his senses. The ice scouring the siding faded to silence until there was only the rustle of her graceful movements, the pad of her step on the carpet. It was too late to hide the card or the emotion leaving him unable to move.

He didn't look up to acknowledge her presence. He could see the black toes of her boots at the far edge of his vision. She'd stopped to lean against the arched doorway. Her nearness breezed over him like a touch against his skin.

"It looks as if we were on the same wavelength."

At the sound of her voice, he dragged his gaze upward. He felt raw, wide open, unable to close down his heart or call up his defenses to protect him from her. The sight of her standing like a dream in the decorated archway, the gentle lights twinkling over her like star shine, took his breath away.

She looked like perfection just standing there, in a simple red sweater and jeans belted at her slim waist, a fuzzy gray cat cradled in her left arm, a small wrapped gift in the other. She arched one eyebrow, awaiting his answer.

His mind was a blur. "What?"

"Exchanging presents. I've got one for you. I'm guessing that one's for me."

Words tore like claws in his throat. Unable to speak, he watched, unable to stop her, as she padded toward him. It felt as if her every step closer was a raw scrape against his exposed heart. Something thudded against the card in his hands. A water droplet. A second. A third. The envelope slid from between his fingers and sailed to the floor, skidding to a halt at Kristin's feet.

"What's this?" She knelt, back straight, keeping the kitty balanced. The paper rasped against the linoleum as she rescued the envelope.

He hung his head, unable to make the wetness in his eyes go away.

Or the explosion inside his heart. What he ought to do was to suck it up, paste a normal look on his face, so she couldn't guess what was going on. Give her the gift, tell her goodbye and march straight into the night. Keep on going until the night numbed him enough so that he could go home, go on with his life per usual.

The card trembled in his hand.

He couldn't let her see. Couldn't let her in. She'd want to soothe him, comfort him with platitudes, and what good would that do? His dad was forever gone. It would never be okay. Never be anything but an unhealed wound inside his heart.

Kristin's hand covered his.

He couldn't look at her. He couldn't talk. He couldn't make himself push her away. The pain swelled in his chest, like a wave breaking against the shore.

"This is from your dad." She sounded gentle. "Where did you get it?"

He scrubbed his eyes, willing the pain away. Failing. "In the pocket. It was his coat."

"Did you read what he wrote?"

He breathed in. His entire being shuddered. Hot grief burned on the back of his eyelids. No, he didn't want to read it. He couldn't bear to bring in any more pain.

He was drowning in it. It did no good to dig up the past. To look back at what could never be changed.

"I think you should." Her words came softly. She held open the card.

He yanked it from her grip. His eyes couldn't focus at first. Head down, he jammed it into his pocket. "I'd best be going."

"You want to open your present first?"

She was remarkable. That's what she was. He swiped his eyes with his fingertips, hiding the fact that his face was wet, and did the best he could to turn away. He felt trapped in purgatory with the past a heavy rock around his neck, drawing him down an endless hill and he was helpless to stop the fall.

"Ryan, you're not okay. Why don't I drive you home?"

He was at the back door. He didn't remember standing up. Walking away. Crossing the room. He leaned his forehead against the cold panel of glass and willed the sob building in his windpipe to stay down. But it was rising up. He couldn't let it.

She was behind him, her hand on his back. A calm steady comfort that he didn't want and couldn't stomach. But he needed it like air.

"No, I'll be fine." He was relieved that his words sounded normal. A little strained, but good enough. He looked down to find Pete's truck keys in his hand. There was nothing to do but leave, while he still had a scrap of dignity. "Merry Christmas, Miss McKaslin."

She slid the gift into his pocket. "Merry Christmas, Dr. Sanders. Drive safe. It's cold out there."

The thick layer of clouds broke apart, sending the snow scattering. A white shaft of moonlight lit the steps ahead, as if to guide him. Kristin watched him slip away, a tall hulk of a man in the parka he didn't bother to zip, and that worried her as she held the door after him.

She could feel the weight of his pain like the press of the frigid air. A pain that staggered her, and as she closed the door, she felt the furnace kick on and the rush of hot air at her ankles. Mickey squirmed in her arms, he wanted down, so she released him.

The grief inside her crescendoed—and it wasn't her own. She could feel his pain. It was odd, as if he were a part of her. She couldn't explain it as she brushed tears from her eyes. *Please, Father, help him to read the card. Comfort him.*

There was no answer as the big shadow of a man ambled down the walkway and toward the garage. He vanished from her sight, but she could feel him still in the center of her heart. So much agony. She rubbed her sternum with the heel of her hand.

Maybe she'd been wrong in letting him go. But he was so capable and he'd stood so strong and straight. As if he didn't need her. Why would he? They weren't even friends, not really.

A blur of movement caught her gaze. There he was, inside Dad's truck. He'd pulled the vehicle out of the garage and, judging by the plume of exhaust, was letting the motor warm up a little before taking off.

The needle on the thermometer tacked on the trunk of the snow-draped maple pointed toward the low minus twenties. Way too cold to take off after him. He sat straight and tall behind the wheel, silhouetted by the slice of moonlight through the clouds. He looked all right.

She didn't know what to do. Only moments ago he'd been seated in the dark, his head bowed, pain radiating off him. She remembered how one drop had marked the card he'd handed her. One tear.

She wasn't sure how to handle that at all. He'd been so restrained then, as he was now, a shadow in the night as he leaned forward, probably to adjust the defroster. He straightened, and the pain inside her swelled until her ribs ached.

Was it her pain? Or his?

Was it possible to feel someone else's emotions?

She didn't know. She stood on tiptoe, trying to see. Ryan's head bowed forward. Was he reading the card? She reached for her coat and let her heart lead her into the cold and night.

Chapter Ten

The past was like a monster reaching out of the dark to choke him. Ryan tossed the child's birthday card on the bench seat. He couldn't look at it. He wasn't a coward or anything, but what was the point? Molten hot emotion built in his chest, threatening to erupt and he couldn't let it. There was no point in giving in to something that couldn't be changed.

What he needed to do was to go home, go to bed, make it through the day and pray for a reason to leave ahead of schedule. Maybe he'd call in for messages. See if there was some emergency he could volunteer for, so he could head home.

He could leave all this behind. Wouldn't that be better? Yeah, he'd give anything right now to be able to be in Phoenix. There were no memories of Dad there. Nor the wild beauty of Montana's icy winters. Just temperate sunshine and rustling palm trees. Yep, that's what he needed.

A knock on the window came out of nowhere—

and sent waves of adrenaline sparking through his veins. The door opened before he could react, and a hooded figure tumbled inside along with the frigid air. Kristin.

"Hey, there." The door shut, and she shivered in her coat and gloves. She didn't appear to notice he wasn't in the mood for company. "I haven't been in this kind of cold since last Christmas. I figure I might as well drive over with you and bring the truck back."

"No way. Then you're out here alone with all this snow. The roads haven't been plowed yet."

"I'm a Montana girl. What's a little snow?"

Silvered by the moonlight, framed by the night, she looked as beautiful as a dream. He swore he could feel more than her physical closeness. Her sympathy, soft as the tiny bit of moonlight reflecting on the miles of snow, chased away the dark. Eased the shadows.

Shame twisted bitterly in his stomach. He couldn't believe how he'd acted in front of her in the kitchen. He'd been way too vulnerable.

Way too…*weak.*

That's what it was. He'd lost his dad as a kid. Sure, it had devastated him, but life went on. Worse tragedies happened every day. He was a man now. A man didn't go around crying like a little boy over what could never be changed. Right?

"Go back in the house, Kristin."

"No. I was feeling lonely tonight, so I thought I'd join you."

"How can I say this nicely? I want to be alone."

"Too bad. Are you going to drive or do you want me to?"

He looked her up and down, as if he wasn't sure what he was going to do.

Kristin's pulse skipped. Was he angry at her? Or was she right in thinking that he was the one who didn't want to be alone? Seconds ticked into minutes as the defroster began to kick out warm air and the clouds overhead sailed in front of the moon, blotting out the light. Leaving only the soft luminescence from the dash controls to see by.

"Stay if you want to." He sounded careless, but he wasn't.

No. Kristin's chest ached with a building pressure. Hurting for him, she opted for silence as he put the truck in gear and hit the headlights. Twin shafts of brightness lit their way as the truck shot forward.

Snow swirled on the ground, drifting, disguising the familiar curve of the driveway. But Ryan forged a path where the road used to be, handling the truck with expert patience whenever the tires lost traction. Without a word, he drove the half mile to his mom's driveway, where the snow had drifted into the cut of the hillside to block the roadway.

He eased the pickup around and pointed her homeward. "I'll hike it the rest of the way."

"It's too cold to walk. You're not dressed for this weather."

"I know what I'm doing. I'll make it in just fine." He set the emergency brake, leaving the truck in neutral. "I don't feel right about letting you drive back."

"I know what I'm doing." She repeated his words. "Apparently we're two people who don't need any help from anyone. Or one another."

That cracked the tension tight around his jaw. A hint of a grin hooked the corner of his mouth. "I'm glad we understand each other."

"Right." She flicked off her hood, since the cab was growing warmer. "Are you going to read your card?"

"That's none of your business."

"True. It's strange, don't you think, that your mom kept your dad's coat—that coat—for so long?"

"I see where you're going with this. And no, Mom's practical. She said to me this morning, before we went out tree cutting, that she knew one day I'd need his coat. The one I brought up from Phoenix wasn't warm enough. That's why she kept it. Just in case. Mom's like that."

"Didn't you notice the card earlier? You could have felt it in the pocket any other time."

"It's a thick goose-down parka. I couldn't tell it was there."

"So why did you find it when you did?"

"Because I was getting your gift out of the pocket. I know what you're doing, and you're wrong. God isn't trying to tell me something. It's a coincidence. It's just a card."

"It's from your father."

He appeared so strong and steady, as if made from granite. A shadow in the darkness, he lifted the card between two fingers and stared at the colorful front, hardly visible in the dash lights, but substantial none-theless.

"I'm done with the past. There's nothing there for me." He stuffed it into his pocket, out of sight.

To be forgotten? Her heart breaking, she felt the wash of his grief. She'd known that devastating pain once, too. Did she tell him what had helped her? Or was he right, that it wasn't her business?

It was as if an angel whispered in her ear and she spoke without knowing what she was saying—she reached across the void between them and brushed a kiss to his cheek. A buzz of sensation flitted through her entire being. The part of her heart that could feel his strengthened.

She leaned back, spinning with the feel of his five o'clock shadow and the clean scent of him. "We're a product of our past. You never accepted your father's death, did you?"

"What was there to accept? It happened. There's nothing I can do to change it."

"No. But you carry that loss with you. I know I do. I wrestled with it for a long time. I just wanted my sister back. My family had fallen apart. Mom had sunk into a depression so deep, we didn't think she'd ever come out. Dad just drifted away. Deciding not to cope at all. He just…kept his distance."

"Sometimes that's the best way. Keep away from what's hurting."

"Yes. That's why I moved to Seattle. Part of the reason." She closed her eyes. Thought of the day that had just passed, different because Allison wasn't there. "Nothing is the same. We've all dealt in our own way. I think my sisters are compensating for the past by marrying and having kids."

"Compensating?"

"Trying to recreate what was lost. We were all so close back then. Our family had a real togetherness. Summer vacations and weekend trips up into the woods to camp. Going to watch both Michelle and Kendra compete—they barrel raced. Friday night gatherings and Saturday horse rides and picnics after church on Sunday. Making snowmen and hiding presents around Christmastime and spending Christmas Eve at the piano while Mom played carol after carol. We'd sing until midnight—"

Grief vised her chest, like an iron band twisting tighter with each breath. "Then there was the plane accident. Allison and Kirby were headed with the church group for a retreat."

"I remember." Ryan's baritone rumbled deep with sorrow. With understanding. "You were lucky Kirby survived."

"We were all so grateful. And at the same time, destroyed. Allison was gone, and our family shattered. As strong as our parents' marriage was, it couldn't stand that loss. And the rest of us just did the best we could. Sometimes the pain feels so fresh. Like on holidays, like tonight. I can't look back because it hurts. I'm sad that nothing is the same. That the future will be forever changed."

Ryan swiped his hand over his face. "Look, I can't do this. I've got to go. Good night."

"Ryan—"

It was beyond rude and he knew it. But he was breaking inside and he had to go. He'd rather face the frigid cold and the hopeless night than to let her in. Let her close. She was coming after him. He could see her in the brief shine of the dome light, which was illuminating the honest compassion on her sweet face. It was too much—too honest, too intimate and too close to breaking open the scars inside him.

He winced as he slammed the door shut, the pain so stark it was as if the grief inside him had broken his ribs. The brief shine from the dome light faded, leaving only the haunting shadow of Kristin, her jaw falling open with surprise at his behavior.

And he hated it. He didn't know what was happening to him. How would someone as perfect as Kristin understand? He sank into snow up to his thigh. Stepped again, cold sliding through his clothes. He cut through the beams of the headlights and faced the dark. Headed to a place that hurt as much as it sheltered. But it was better than going back, although something inside him felt stretched, as if an unseen force was pulling him back. Holding on. Never letting go.

Was it Kristin? Why could he still feel her kiss on his cheek? Not even the icy wind was able to numb the tingle on his skin. The night could not diminish the glow in his spirit when he thought of her.

Look after her, Father. Please. Ryan couldn't turn

around, but he could feel her watching him. Praying for him. He had to keep going—it felt as if his survival depended on it. On putting as much distance as he could away from her. Away from her kindness. Her caring. Her softness.

How had she gotten so deep into his soul? He only knew he didn't want her there. He didn't want anyone that close. He tromped through the drifting snow, sinking and struggling. It was tough going, but he didn't care. He just wanted as far away from her as he could get. His heart was bursting, his spirit fracturing and he was thankful when the shadows swallowed him from Kristin's sight. He heard the truck's idle change—she was shifting into gear. The increased hum of the engine reverberated through the silent night as she gave it enough gas to pull out onto the lonely road and then the sound faded into nothing.

Only then did he turn and watch the faint beam of taillights grow smaller in the vast darkness until they disappeared. He was alone, and the bitter cold hadn't eased the agony inside him. Hadn't erased the grip Kristin had on his soul.

With his step crunching on the new snow, Ryan's breathing came loud as the night seemed to draw more silent. As if it lay in quiet anticipation. He'd never heard such silence. Endless and echoing and hushed.

By the time he'd made it to the back steps, he was frozen clear through. His hands and feet were numb. His face chapped and burning. The card and gift in his pocket felt like lead weights, growing heavier with every step he took.

He'd been so wrong to run to her tonight. That's what he'd done, wasn't it? Hauling his tail through a storm to the warmth of her presence. Why had he done it? It had made sense at the time, but now—now everything was worse.

Grateful for the porch light guiding him in, he stumbled up the buried porch steps, kicking snow away as he went. It had drifted up against the back door, even though Mom had probably cleared it away before she went to bed. He grabbed the shovel leaning against the siding and gave a few swipes to clear a path.

Not that the inside of this house was a sanctuary. If anything, his chest hurt worse. His heart broke apart even more. He kicked out of his boots, his numbed feet feeling thick and unresponsive. His fingers were no better. He headed straight to the woodstove in the corner, which crackled and popped as it radiated wonderful heat.

Unzipping, he sank onto the hot floor bricks and let the warmth wash over him like bliss. He was so cold, he couldn't feel it. His entire body started to shiver.

Okay, he'd been desperate to go out in the cold dressed like he was. Even his bones felt frozen. He thought of Kristin when he climbed to his feet. The clock said ten minutes to midnight. That meant she ought to be just about home now. The roads were pretty much impassable. He never should have agreed to let her come. If he'd been in more control of his emotions, he certainly wouldn't have allowed such a thing.

And at this late hour, he couldn't call and wake up the entire house to make sure she was safe.

Worry churned through him. He grabbed a cup from the cupboard and filled it with water, hating his clumsy movements. He heated water in the microwave and dug through the drawers until he found where Mom kept the tea. She had a whole drawer full of different boxes of the stuff.

He grabbed a fruity-flavored one, dunked the bag in the steaming water. Just cupping it in his hands made him feel warmer. He drank it right there in one long draw and refilled the cup and nuked it again.

He felt marginally better. Still shivering, the minute and a half it took for the machine to ding felt like an eternity. He watched the wall clock's hands move closer to midnight.

The ringing phone surprised him. With adrenaline still knocking through him, he grabbed the receiver before it could ring again. "Kristin?"

"Just checking to make sure you made it indoors safely," she answered.

Relief slid through him that she was also okay. He stopped quaking. Then again, it might have been from the hot tea. The microwave dinged in the background. He couldn't think of what to say other than, *Sorry I was a moron and ran off like that. Sorry I couldn't handle finding a piece of paper in my pocket.*

But she spoke, breaking the silence between them. "Well, I just wanted to ease my mind. I had visions of you frozen in a snowbank in midstride. When I got home, the thermometer read twenty-four below. I shouldn't have let you walk off like that."

"The driveway was full of drifts. The truck would have gotten stuck. Did you have any problems?"

"Nope."

She sounded sad, and he hated that. Ryan took a second to gather up his courage. "I left kind of quick back there."

"It's okay. I overstepped. You're right. I never should have—"

Ryan's conscience winced. He didn't want her to go blaming herself when it was all his fault. His failings. Hadn't Francine done the same thing? Always trying to be there for him, when he couldn't take the pain of letting anyone that close?

He was wrong. "No, you were great. You were a good friend tonight. I just— I just handle things on my own. It's the way I am."

"Okay." She sounded relieved, less strained. "You take care of yourself. And have a good Christmas with your family."

"You, too." His windpipe collapsed and he could barely get out a goodbye before he hung up. The phone cord dangled long and coiled up, the way it always used to.

The years rolled back against his will and he could remember his dad standing right here, hand on the receiver as he hung up, the last time Ryan had seen him. How big and strong and manly his dad was, the quiet capable type. Dad's deep gravelly voice seemed to rumble through the years and echo all around Ryan.

He saw the past and the present at the same time. The

shadowed room where the fire sparkled in the tempered window of the woodstove. The little boy's view looking up at his dad, who was saying they had the prescription ready in town, he'd be back with it and their favorite carton of ice cream. *You be a good boy for your mom, and I'll be right back. We'll get some medicine in you, and you'll be feeling better soon. I promise.*

The darkness swallowed him and Ryan sank to his knees. The hard edges of the brick hearth bit into his kneecaps. Knowing it would break him forever, he pulled the card from his pocket. When he opened the envelope, the orange-and-black cast from the fire writhed upon the page. There was Dad's writing from the past filling the present. *I love you, son.*

The weight of the past broke free. *I love you, too, Dad.* Hot waves of sorrow crashed through him. *I just want you back.* He fought to hold on, but he couldn't. Tears burned in his eyes and brimmed. The first sob escaped, scraping painfully up his throat. A second. A third.

He buried his face in his hands, which were no longer numb. Hurting with a heart that was no longer shielded.

Christmas came with a whisper. The wall clock gently bonged once, as if in welcome. Ryan ignored it. He'd never felt more hopeless or alone.

He didn't see the tiniest bits of snow begin to drift down from the black velvet sky. They were delicate flakes, crested by starlight and glowing like hope.

As if God were listening on this wintry, holy night.

* * *

Kristin waited until the final chime of the grandfather clock in the living room silenced. Christmas came on the wings of snow that fell in dazzling reassurance to the frozen ground. Starlight eased between the breaks in the clouds to make the fields surrounding the house shimmer like an opal. Wetness burned in her eyes, and she couldn't say why.

Maybe she was tired. Maybe it was stress. Or the worry over what tomorrow would bring.

So many worries weighed down on her.

It was Ryan and the way he'd practically leaped out of the truck and run away as fast as he could plow through the snow. How could she blame him? She'd leaned across the seat and kissed him. She'd done it without thinking, on impulse. She'd never done such a thing before. She'd called him to apologize, and had lost the nerve to say, "Sorry I threw myself at you."

She wrapped her arms around her middle. It was her family, and worrying about tomorrow, which was already here. Christmas, alive and solemn.

Snapshots from Christmases past clustered the end wall in the breezeway. She stopped to study them. Framed in gold, reflecting the wink of the tree lights, she looked at the past. At the scrawny little girl with her long hair and straight-edged bangs, thanks to Mom's home cut. She sat in the middle, surrounded by all her sisters, crowding close with the Christmas tree in the background. They were all beaming from their exciting morning of ripping open Santa's gifts.

Each year Mom had framed a similar snapshot of the six of them crowded together in front of the tree. Happy and laughing. Allison, the tallest, was always in the back of their group. Slim and sleek and beautiful. She'd been kind and good every day of her life. There were so many pictures without her.

There was last year's picture—just the five of them. Mom always wanted a snapshot of her girls. But in the corner of the frame, there was another. The grandchildren in their new Christmas clothes for church. They'd gathered here and snapped the Polaroid in front of the tree. Mom must have taken several, reserving one to tuck in this frame.

Life was going on, rolling like the earth in the universe. Tugged along on a path that could not be stopped. It hurt, what was left behind.

She went to wipe the dampness from her eyes and the shocking sound of the mugs clinking together startled her. She'd forgotten she was holding them in her left hand, lost in her thoughts when she should be shutting down the house for the night.

She unplugged Christmas lights in the kitchen. Rinsed the cups and tucked them into the top dishwasher rack. Watched the colorful lights hooked over the bay window valances blink out as she hit the switch. Something moved out of the corner of her eye, a rustle of movement. One of the cats?

She checked the cushions on the window seat. No feline was hiding there or beneath the table. Strange. For some reason the cushions looked inviting and she eased down on them. Ryan's gift, as small as a jewelry box, sat on the center of the table, where he'd left it.

She'd forgotten about it until now. The silver-and-gold wrapping was crumpled in one corner, and the frilly bow was squished from being in his pocket.

Ryan. She wished she could rewind time like a tape and replay it. What had he said? That she'd been a good friend. A friend. That was nice. Maybe he didn't hold her impulsive kiss against her.

So, what had he gotten her? She removed the bow and set it aside, tugging the ribbon until it unraveled. She lifted the lid and gasped. Elegant gold dangle earrings in the shape of snowflakes glinted in the faint starlight. Oh, this was too much, it was too expensive—

A small card was inside, too. She pulled it out. He'd written, *To the storm that brought old acquaintances together and made us friends.*

Yes, that felt right. *Friends.* The warm glow in her spirit remained. As if a door had opened to a place within her heart. To what, she didn't know. Ryan lived in Phoenix. She lived in Seattle. The most they could be would be long-distance friends. It seemed as if the only thing they had in common were their visits home for the holidays.

On the wide wooden sill behind her, the delicate porcelain figures sat in eternal worship. The barn animals, the wise men and mother and father. All knelt before the simple manger where the Christ child lay.

Her breath fogged on the cold window, but she couldn't move. Couldn't look away. Cold radiated through the windows. Warmth from the heat vent curled around her ankles. Tiny snowflakes flitted against the window.

Slowly the grief inside her ebbed away, leaving in its place peace.

Chapter Eleven

Christmas Day

Kristin's cell phone rang. Yanking her favorite Christmas sweater over her head, she dug through her bag on the floor until she found it. She checked the ID on the screen before answering. "Hey, Karen. How did Allie like her trike?"

"She's squealing and pedaling around the living room as we speak. I tried to get her off to eat breakfast and she raised such a fuss, I just handed her a waffle and let her eat and drive."

"Sounds like it was a hit. Did Zach tell you how hard that thing was to put together?"

"Yep. 'Santa' is still assembling some of the other toys. He's been at it since sunup." Karen's voice sparkled with happiness. In the background, a little girl's squeals of delight rang like merry bells, accompanied by a loud crash. "Oops, I gotta go. Disasters abound. I'll see you around noon. Merry Christmas!"

She sounded so happy, Kristin thought as she tucked her phone into her back jean pocket. Good. Karen, who'd been closest to Allison, had a hard time with her death. Now, she was laughing and happy again. That was a good thing. But Kristin couldn't help worrying. She prayed Karen had one of those special marriages that would last. She wished that for all her sisters.

She didn't know how they could do it, but she was thankful they were all thriving and content.

She hopped over Minnie, asleep on the sunny landing, and down the stairs. Presents were heaped under the lit tree, and the fragrance of wood smoke and fresh pine was like every other Christmas in her memory. She followed the scent of sizzling bacon to the kitchen, where Mom was at the stove, spatula in hand.

"Merry Christmas. Is Dad in the barn?"

"Yes, indeed. The snow had drifted over the back door and he had to dig his way out. What a storm we must have had last night." Mom flipped the bacon, the hollows beneath her eyes, bruised with exhaustion, told a different story. "Did you want one egg or two?"

"Are you kidding? Two. It's not every day I get treated to your eggs Benedict." She kissed her mom's cheek as she slipped by.

Mickey was purring, content to lie on the heat register beneath the table. She stooped to give him a stroke, wondering. Mom looked so worn out, as if she hadn't slept at all. And what about Dad?

A knock at the back door—it was Dad. He poked his head in, his skin was red from the cold. His lined plaid hat with the earflaps was dappled with ice pellets. "Kris—get your boots on and help me. The water's froze up solid at the barn."

"Are the animals all right?"

"For now, but that heater conked out sometime during the night. Don't know how long they've been without water. We've got to start packin'."

"Okay." She reached for her coat, unhooking it from the back closet. The frigid draft from the partially opened door had her shivering. She dug through the closet for insulated gloves. There had to be an extra pair lying around somewhere.

"Pete." Mom's voice felt as chilled as the outside air. "Will you be long? I've just put the eggs on."

"Well, now, I don't rightly know, Alice." Dad sounded tired. Irritable. "It'll take as long as it takes. You know that."

Her parents arguing—it used to be a rare thing. She hated it. Her stomach clenched tight. *Please, stop,* she wished with all her might.

But Mom didn't. She kept right on going. "It'll ruin the eggs to keep them warming."

"What would you have me do? You'll just have to wait, Alice." With a tired sigh, Dad closed the door with a click that echoed through the tense silence in the kitchen.

Kristin released a shaky breath. That was why she never wanted to get married. If her parents, who'd had the perfect marriage and life together, couldn't make love last, then no one could. From the outside, they looked content enough. But behind closed doors, the distance and the hurt separated them. How long would it be until the anger progressed to bitter hatred? Would they divorce?

Her stomach burned. No, that was unthinkable. Her parents wouldn't do that. They wouldn't walk away from their holy vows in that final way. She jerked on the pair of gloves she'd found. They were too big, probably an extra pair of Dad's.

What difference did it make? She just wanted outside. She was choking, and Mom was muttering to herself as she put the eggs on to cook. Words that Kristin didn't want to hear. Turning away, she pounded outside and into the brutal cold before she realized she hadn't zipped up.

She didn't even remember pulling her coat on. Ice dried on her cheeks as she bent to zip up, the thick gloves making it difficult.

No, her parents wouldn't divorce, she realized as she looked around at the sprawling home and well-kept outbuildings, at the horses milling around the open barn doors. Mom and Dad had built something good here together. They wouldn't divide it up into his and hers. They'd just live like this forever, silently angry and quietly hurting.

Marriage was such a blessing? Not from where she stood. Disillusionment twisted in her heart on this most sacred of mornings. She tried to push it aside but she couldn't. Since Dad had left two ten-gallon buckets by the back steps, she swept them off and sidled back inside to the laundry room, off the mudroom, where she hefted the buckets into the oversize sink and hit the faucet.

There was no way she was ever going to get married. No way she was ever going to trust that one day her world wouldn't be pulled out from under her like a rug beneath her feet. Leaving her in pieces and hurting as Mom was. She tried not to listen to the sounds of Mom's anger. The harsh ring of a pot or the harder than necessary thud of a cupboard door closing

The buckets were nearly full. Kristin, used to the drill, turned off the water, hiked the buckets with care and lugged them to the back door. It felt like a two-mile trek to the barn hauling twenty gallons of water. Her nose, throat and lungs burned from the icy wind as she struggled across the backyard. Dad had broken a path, but she still sank into snow up to the top of her boots.

"Say, thanks for your help, Kris." There was Dad, hurrying to take the heavy load from her.

He was such a kind man. Why couldn't he and Mom just get along?

"I've got a space heater working in the utility room. Temporary fix." Dad gestured with a curt nod toward the corner room, where the water heater and industrial furnace were housed. "Could you do me a favor? Run in the house, would ya, and fetch my phone. I left it in the living room."

She heard what he didn't say. He didn't want to face Mom. "Fine. I'll do that."

"Good. I figure all our little ones are up by now. All that excitement with Santa Claus comin', you know." His blue eyes twinkled and for a moment he looked young and alive. But the brightness slipped away and left a tired, aging man. An unhappy man.

"I might as well warn the boys I'll be needin' their help today. Sure is good havin' them in the family. You wouldn't be lookin' to give me another son-in-law, would you?"

"Dad! Not you, too." She snatched up empty buckets from the ground, ones Dad had just emptied. "I expected better from you."

"I'm just sayin'. It doesn't hurt to mention it." Dad upended a full bucket over the top of the gate and into his mare's water trough. "Noticed you and Ryan are getting close."

"We're *friends*. You know. We're *friendly*."

"Well, sure, but he'd make a fine son-in-law. He's smart, works hard, respectful to women and his elders. It'd be awful handy to have a doctor in the family."

"Dad! I'd much rather haul twenty gallons of water in the freezing cold than stand here and listen to this." With the buckets she held clanking, she marched straight to the door without looking back.

Although she couldn't stop from wondering—why was her dad doing this, too? Putting so much attention on her and Ryan's friendship that could never be anything more.

Maybe because it helped them to forget for a while their own unhappiness.

Snow tickled her nose as she negotiated the treacherous path to the house. She could see Mom through the big bay window busy at the stove, the bow of her apron at the small of her back. Her left shoulder hitched high to keep the phone at her ear while she worked. Probably hearing about her grandchildren.

Kristin popped open the door to the sound of Mom's voice, falsely cheerful.

"Oh, I'm sure Allie will get the hang of it in no time… I suppose the couch will have to face a few more head-on accidents before the day is through. How's little Anna? Loves to rip the paper…"

Talking with Karen, Kristin concluded, as she elbowed into the laundry room and set the buckets in the sink. Bits of conversation rose over the rush of the water. "Oh, dear, Kirby's calling on the other line. Yes, I'll tell her. See you in a bit… Kirby, Merry Christmas. Michael did *what?*" Mom laughed, shallow and forced, the note ringing hollow on this holy day.

The tension between her and Dad lingered.

Once they'd all come together in celebration and joy. Christmas would never be that way again. Her family was forever changed.

Ryan followed his nose down the hall, yawning. He wasn't even really awake yet, but his stomach was growling. He shuffled in his socks and his flannel pj's, lured by the scents of coffee and sausage and maple syrup.

"Hey, sleepyhead." Mom sat in her favorite chair by

the window, smiling up at him as her knitting needles flashed. "Mia's still asleep, too. Boy, does this take me back to when you two were teenagers on a weekend morning."

"Weekends and holidays are made for sleeping in. You know that." He raked a hand through his hair. Yawned again. He was still tired. He couldn't say he got much sleep last night.

Christmas was everywhere. The solemn carols humming from the little stereo system he'd gotten Mom for her last birthday. The blink and glisten of the tree lights. The presents piled beneath the branches. A mix of the presents for each other and ones "Santa" had left overnight. The serene glow of love that lingered in this house. Why hadn't he noticed that before?

"I have your breakfast keeping warm in the oven. Don't forget to rinse your plate!"

"Yeah, yeah." He stooped to brush a kiss to her forehead. "Merry Christmas."

Mom's eyes filled. "Oh, you're my favorite son."

"I'm your only son, but I am your favorite." He winked, enjoying the sound of her chuckle as he left the room. One thing about his mom, she loved both Mia and him equally. But he was uncomfortable with what he'd wanted to say. Like, I love you, Mom.

With the fire snapping in the woodstove, the kitchen was blissfully warm. He found two plates keeping warm in the oven, the smaller one was Mia's. He took the big serving plate, heaped with scrambled eggs, pancakes and sausage links to the table.

It was a very white Christmas. Snow clouds rolled along the sky like waves in an ocean, undulating and white-capped and stunning, crashing upon the frosted mountains. The roll of land, the draw of valley and silent firs snowcapped and still, tugged at his heart, summoning the past. Memories surged through him. Of Dad at the table, nose in the paper as he dragged out that last cup of coffee and used the last sausage link to wipe up the puddle of maple syrup from the pancakes.

Mom, younger and more lively, taking the empty plate from him. "No, you just relax. You work enough for two men the week through."

Mia hopping up from the table—spritelike and freckle-faced as she'd been as a little girl. "I wanna open the presents now. Can we? Can we?"

"After your father finishes his coffee," Mom had answered from the sink. "Ryan, are you still eating? Haven't you filled that hollow leg of yours yet? There's one more pancake. Go ahead and eat it."

That had been their last Christmas together, Ryan remembered as he sat down to the table with the syrup bottle in hand. He'd gotten skis as part of his cache and after Christmas dinner, Dad had taken him outside. Showed him how to cross-country.

The years fell away and he was an eight-year-old bundled well in bulky winter gear. The thick scarf and the parka's hood made it hard to tip his head back far enough to look up at his dad. Dad had seemed so tall and invincible. A superhero of a man who could do anything.

With endless patience, Dad showed him how to use the poles to kick off and glide. "With a little practice, you'll be good enough to go up in the backcountry with me."

"Can I, can I?"

"Sure thing, Son. I promise. We'll make a day of it. We'll use the new binoculars you and your sister got me. I bet we'll even see a few wildcat tracks, if we're lucky."

A promise that Dad never got to keep.

Ryan could almost feel the pure thrill of anticipation he'd felt that Christmas. How like a man he felt skiing alongside his dad. Being big enough to get to go up into the mountains. Of swelling up with love until he'd felt like bursting, as his dad's hand came to rest on his shoulder.

"That's my boy," Dad had said.

In the warmth of the kitchen, Ryan took a steadying breath. His vision was blurry, and he swore he could feel the weight of his dad's hand on his shoulder still. Could still sense his father's love and pride.

Something he hadn't felt since that long-ago day.

Why? He'd never faced his grief before. He'd been a kid. He hadn't known how to handle his father's death. And through the years, it had been easier to push those feelings down. Until last night. Until he'd found the card.

Because of Kristin. She was the reason. If his mom hadn't been trying to fix him up with her and arranged for them to cut Christmas trees, then he wouldn't have used Dad's coat. And he wouldn't have put Kristin's gift in the pocket where the forgotten card had resided.

Kristin. He thought about her. About how she'd looked last night in the truck's dome light, full of compassion and caring and beauty. How she was like the gentle peace of a winter morning, and he wanted to see her. He missed her company. There was a place deep in his heart that warmed. It was like the connection he'd felt last night between them, and he wondered if she was thinking of him, too.

Oblivious to the tension in the living room, little golden-haired Allie galloped in circles around the couch, holding on to her new toy horses with real manes, who were "galloping" with her. Her little sister, Anna, ran after her with one hand outstretched and the other clutching the couch for balance, making a shrill sound of glee.

Kristin moved her left foot in time to save it from being run over by little Michael's dump truck that raced on the edge of the cold hearth bricks. With the help of Michael's sound effects and guiding hand, the truck took a tragic head-on into the wood box, flew through the air to roll to a stop where Kristin's foot used to be.

"Uh-oh!" Baby Emily commented as she hugged her Sesame Street doll that was laughing hysterically.

Wearing a very fashionable red-and-green Christmas sleeper that said Santa's Favorite in candy-cane striping, Baby Caitlin yawned, stretched her little fists and nestled deeper into her mommy's arms. Seated side by side, Kendra and her husband Cameron watched their infant daughter sleep with sheer love on their faces.

Kristin prayed that their love would last. She wished that for all of her sisters. And for her parents, who sat on opposite sides of the room, Mom staring at the brochure that held the tickets and paid hotel-and-tour vouchers. That wish was looking more and more like an impossibility.

"Look what the girls got us, Pete." Mom held up the picture of a lush Maui resort.

Mom didn't look too happy. Kristin glanced at her sister Michelle, who was seated on the chair next to her.

"Disaster," Michelle leaned over to whisper.

"Uh-oh!" Emily commented from Michelle's lap.

Exactly. Kristin watched as Mom struggled to smile. Not a real smile. And the last of Kristin's hopes—and, she was sure, all of her sisters'—broke into a thousand pieces.

"Well, now," Dad commented as even the children silenced. "That was real thoughtful of you girls."

"You always used to talk about a second honeymoon in Hawaii, but with the running of the farm, there was never any time," Kirby gently explained. "So we thought— well…"

"Since you never got the chance to go," Michelle broke in. "We'd help you along. Merry Christmas."

"That's real fine." Dad's smile was too tight, but he was trying to be gracious.

As Karen and Kirby huddled around Mom, showing her all that the two-week vacation included, Dad stood from his recliner and began clearing away the wrapping paper. Brody and Cameron got up to help him. The TV flashed to life. Little Michael had abandoned his dump truck to take command of the remote control.

Sam blew a raspberry on his boy's cheek and they chuckled together, father and son. "If you're going to take charge of the remote, you've got to make sure to turn it to football. That's it, hit that button right there. Good boy."

The black-and-white Jimmy Stewart movie switched to a game in progress. The men froze, staring at the screen as a football sailed through the air—

"Incomplete!" the commentator announced and the men moaned in agony.

"How badly do you think we goofed?" Michelle whispered, keeping one eye on Mom. "I should never have pushed for this. I just want them to be happy."

"That's what we all want. We want our mom and dad back the way they were. In love again." Love, once lost, could never be found. That's what Kristin was beginning to see for certain. "You meant well, and it was a great idea. Everybody thought so."

"I'm still holding out hope. I say they'll go on this second honeymoon and fall madly in love the way they used to be. It, like, happens in movies and stuff."

"Uh-oh!" Emily shrieked, just for the fun of it.

My thoughts exactly. Kristin knew all too well the look of suppressed pain on her mother's face. A second honeymoon was the last thing her parents wanted. Maybe their love had finished for good, and they would settle for distant indifference for the rest of their married lives.

Sad. Kristin's stomach clenched so tight, she winced.

"I thought it was a fine idea!" Gramma sidled in behind them. "Just what they need. Once they spend their first evening dining on their lanai gazing out at that tropical sunset, they'll thank you. You wait and see. Kris, who gave you those earrings? They're just lovely."

"A friend." A friend she'd been trying not to think about all day.

"Oh? Which friend?"

"Ooh, Gramma, she won't tell us!" Michelle protested. "I asked. Kirby asked. Karen asked. Kendra asked. Mom asked. She just gets that panicked look on her face, which can only mean one thing. It's from a man friend. A *boyfriend!*"

"No! I never said that." Kristin knew she was walking the edge of a lie, but—

"I heard you and Ryan Sanders were spending time together." Gramma seemed so pleased. "First you spend time with him when you were home at Thanksgiving—"

"We drove together. We didn't go out on a date—"

"And now he's giving you expensive jewelry. Of course he's only a friend." Gramma was beaming as she scooped Emily from Michelle's arms. "Come to great-gramma, precious girl."

"Those are expensive-looking earrings." Michelle chimed in appreciation. "Ryan sure must like you."

Kristin leaped out of the chair. It wasn't because she was panicked. "I think I hear the phone ringing."

"You know what Gramma says. One day the love bug's gonna bite you. Watch out, sister dear!"

"Yeah, maybe I have immunity to the love-bug bite." Kristin escaped while she could into the kitchen where the whir of the dishwasher was a welcome relief. Alone, she grabbed a can of diet cola from the fridge.

Ryan. She'd been trying to keep him out of her mind all day. That couldn't be a good sign. Had she ever thought about a man so often? Not in all her life. Not once. What could that mean?

"Oh, Kristin. Would you mind taking out the pies? Your dad is asking for dessert." Mom padded in and pulled a knife and a pie server from the utensil drawer. She looked so sad, even when she smiled.

If only there was something she could do. She set aside the can of soda to give her mom a hug. In the twinkle lights of the kitchen, with the sounds of Christmas all around, Kristin was grateful for her mom and her dad. Grateful for their health and prosperity. Thankful for the family that filled this house.

"I told Kendra I'd bring out the high chair." Mom hurried away, busy as always, leaving Kristin alone.

As she was setting out the homemade chocolate-cream pies, the phone rang. The TV blared as the Cowboys gained four more yards on their second down. The men in the living room cheered, drowning out the sound of a bell ringing.

The phone. Kristin reached for the receiver, then

waited. The caller ID said Sanders. Was it Ryan? Or his mom? Over the noise in the living room, no one else heard the phone ring three more times. Kristin waited in the glow of the twinkle lights as the recorder beeped to life.

"Hey," came Ryan's smooth baritone, deep and wonderful. "Merry Christmas, McKaslin family. I'm trying to get a hold of Kristin. I'll be in town until Saturday night. Give me a call. There's the matter of a chocolate milkshake we need to discuss. Okay? Bye."

She could really like him. Maybe she already liked him too much. The tug of pain in her chest, deep in her heart, was regret. Not love. The connection she felt to him wasn't what she wanted at all. She refused to get carried away and let caring turn to something more dangerous. She had to stop this and stop it now.

She hit the Erase button, wiped away the evidence of Ryan's call, yet the link remained. It was a glow in the center of her chest that didn't fade but remained long into the night as she lay awake, listening to the wind at the eaves.

A fitful sleep claimed her and, when she awoke with the dawn, still the connection stirred within her.

Chapter Twelve

December 31

Ryan hit the lights the minute he walked in the kitchen door. His keys landed on the tile counter and his shoes echoed in the quiet room as he glanced through the mail. A few bills, his school loan payment, an invite to some charity event and the flier from his local church. The last envelope in his hand froze him in place.

It was from his friend Mark, at the clinic in the Seattle area. The one he'd interviewed with in November. He ran his thumb over the tasteful embossed blue-and-green lettering of the return address. Mark had e-mailed him yesterday. Said they were still shorthanded and had a growing practice. They sure would be interested in bringing him on board.

Yeah. He was more interested than ever. His trip home for Christmas had wound up changing everything. Not that he would ever stop missing his dad, and nothing would ever stop the pain of losing his father. But at least he could remember the good times. Like the sun through storm clouds, there was light, and it was easier to see a lot of things he hadn't before.

He liked Phoenix, but he missed the seasons. He missed being able to ski without hopping into a plane first. He wanted to be closer to his mom. She wasn't getting any younger.

Seattle was green and tidy and metropolitan enough to give him a choice in his work. It was located on the water. He could boat, windsurf and ride a Jet Ski during the summers. In less than an hour's drive, he could be on the slopes in winter.

It was a fairly short flight to Montana. He could pay for his mom to visit as much as she wanted.

And, best of all, he already had friends in the area. Jeremiah and Mark and Kristin. Kristin lived in Seattle.

What was he going to do about Kristin? He pulled the folded tie out of his jacket pocket. The colorful sails of the sailboats and Windsurfers soared on a soft blue background. It had been Kristin's Christmas gift to him. He wore it today and thought of her. Nearly every minute of the day.

She'd never returned his call on Christmas. He'd left two messages the next day and nothing.

No. He'd messed that up. He'd pushed her away deliberately that night he'd fled from the truck, when she'd been offering him her help. Her friendship. Maybe more.

He'd blown it, like he always did. He'd been alone for so long, deliberately keeping people away, maybe he didn't know how to do anything else.

Maybe that was for the best.

He wandered into the bedroom, wondering. Maybe he'd make a few calls on Monday. Find out if this offer was in his best interests. What would it cost him to move? He'd have to arrange for movers and look for a new residence to rent or buy. And his work—he had surgery scheduled out two months. He couldn't move before then.

It was a lot to consider.

He grabbed the remote off the corner of the dresser, where the housekeeper always placed it when she'd been in. The silent TV burst to life and a fireworks celebration exploded across the scene. He glanced at the clock. It was four minutes into the new year.

It felt like a new beginning. What was ahead of him for the coming year? he wondered. Would he find real happiness?

With her stomach in knots, Kristin snapped off the small TV in her living room and the New Year's festivities on the East Coast faded into black. Minnie, drowsing on the back of the couch, slit one eye as she passed by.

The kitchen was dark. She made her way to the microwave by memory after grabbing her favorite mug and filling it with water. Her nightly ritual—she heated the mug and water and grabbed a bag of her favorite chamomile tea. The luminous green numbers on the stove told her how late it was. Where was Michelle? She should have called by now.

As if in answer, the phone rang and she snatched it up. "Please, don't tell me they refused to go."

"Okay, I won't." Michelle sounded cheerful. That had to be a good sign. "Brody and I drove them to the airport. They got on the plane this morning as planned. But I got some really awesome news and I spent the rest of the day at Kirby's place."

"What kind of awesome news?"

"She and Sam decided to wait to tell everyone, until they knew for sure and there were no complications. But she's—"

"Pregnant?"

"With twins, thanks to in vitro! Isn't that totally cool? I mean, imagine Christmas next year. My little one will be here. Kirby's twins will be here. Isn't it totally amazing? Remember how sad it used to be, after Allison left us?"

"I remember. Nothing was ever right again."

"But now it's like that's healing. We're all married and starting our own families. It's like coming full circle. Well, except for you. You're the last holdout."

"And that's a plan I intend to stick to."

"Sure, okay. Be stubborn. I'm sure when God's ready He'll send the perfect Mr. Right into your life. If He hasn't already."

"Stop that! You're sounding way too happy. I like being on my own."

"Good. But being married to your soul mate is *so*

much better. You'll see. Anyway, maybe this trip alone together is exactly what Mom and Dad need. True love can heal anything. Don't you think?"

No. Kristin didn't believe in true love. Not anymore. But it was a nice thought, and Michelle had always been optimistic. Maybe that's why she had the courage to marry—she imagined the best that could be.

Where Kristin was too much of a realist. "I'm certainly praying that it does."

"Ooh, me, too! Oh, there's Emily. I gotta go. Happy New Year! Later…"

The microwave dinged, an echoing beep that emphasized the silence and the shadows. Kristin popped the door and set the tea bag to steep in the steaming water. See how quiet it was here? How calm? How safe? Love wasn't safe, that was for sure. It wasn't sure and solid at all. She hoped Mom and Dad could find their love for one another again, but she didn't believe they would.

All it had taken was one tragedy to rip their world apart. Kristin had never recovered from Allison's death, either. She'd found a way to go on. Learned from that hard life experience that people of faith weren't immune to tragedy. It was a part of life. But you could make good common-sense choices. You could be smart and protect yourself.

That's why she was happy here. Maybe not blissful, the way her sisters were, but the upside was that she wouldn't experience the deep lows that her siblings might encounter one day. The fall into despair. The life she'd built for herself was a sensible one. She owned this lovely home, modest, but a sound investment. She'd built equity and refinanced with an incredible interest rate. She worked hard, spent her money wisely and had built a very sound savings making a solid rate in bonds and CDs.

Yes, she had a good practical life. One that made her content. And content was enough. It had to be.

And Ryan? Well, she'd tucked his earrings away in her jewelry box. She'd added him to her prayers, wishing for him the best possible future. But she wasn't going to let her regard for him turn into anything as untrustworthy as love.

No, she was better off alone. That's the way she liked it.

January 19

Ryan's day could have gone better. Two hours behind schedule, he was stuck in traffic in the middle of one of Seattle's floating bridges. The barely measurable forward progress he was making in the left lane had stalled to a dead stop for the last twenty-three minutes.

The downpour turned torrential, and he flicked the windshield wipers on high. Hit the brake. Great. Now the traffic wasn't moving at all. His interview had gone way late, but it had gone well. He liked the clinic and their philosophy, and their waterfront offices were a definite bonus. He'd even checked out the affiliated hospital. It was all great, but it had taken time.

He had a seven-fifteen flight. If the traffic was going

to be uncooperative, then he wouldn't have time to look up Kristin.

The truth was, he was almost glad. Maybe the problem had solved itself. He'd been struggling with whether to call her, or whether to let their so-called friendship go.

He tugged Mom's letter from his coat pocket and unfolded it, keeping one eye on the road, but the traffic was gridlocked. A gust of wind roared around the car and the concrete and steel beneath the car shook from the force. White-capped waves sloshed over the concrete barrier.

He studied the numbers she'd sent. Kristin's home, work and cell-phone numbers. He certainly had the information he needed to contact her. Should he? Or would she refuse to take his call again?

He didn't know what he felt. He didn't know what he wanted. He only knew that the thought of calling her and seeing her again made his palms sweat. Nerves. Anxiety. Stress.

He'd leave it up to heaven to decide. If the traffic started moving, and he had enough time to see her, he'd call. Easy as that. But if the traffic stayed like this, he'd creep and crawl right on past the downtown high-rises.

An hour later, he had his answer. Twilight came and he'd moved to the far side of the bridge. Rush hour had officially started. He crumpled Mom's letter and tossed it into the car's little plastic garbage bag.

Problem solved.

April 11

"Do I have the best sisters, or what?" Michelle swiped her eyes as she gazed around the coffee shop decorated for a baby shower. "Oh, look at me. I'm bawling again. Oh, I didn't expect this. I thought it was Bible Study as usual. You fooled me!"

"No, we surprised you." Kristin wrapped her arm around Michelle's slim shoulders and guided her to the chair reserved just for her. "You told me you would be needing all new things for this baby."

"I did!" Michelle glowed as she eased into the chair, her hand rubbing her swollen tummy that looked ready to burst beneath her pink maternity T-shirt. "Oh, this blue comforter set is so wonderful, Kristin."

"It's from all of us." Karen circled behind the counter with a tray of iced drinks. "Your favorite Italian soda. Oh, and there's Mary's car driving up. Kristin, would you help her carry in the food?"

"Sure." More than happy to let her sister show off the new crib set, Kristin escaped out the front door and into the warm spring day. She loved her sisters, but she'd already been asked about Ryan nearly two-dozen times since she'd arrived yesterday. That was two-dozen times too many.

"Kristin." It was his voice. Had she imagined it?

No, there he was, rising up from behind his mom's sensible sedan. He looked *good*. Bronzed with a tan as if he'd been getting more time out of the office. Unlike he'd been at Christmas, he looked relaxed. At ease.

Her heart hitched hard, and it hurt to breathe. He was the last man she wanted to see. How could Karen have sent her out here? Had her sisters done it on purpose?

He held a covered pot in his broad hands. "I'm the

official Crock-Pot carrier. My mom appointed me. I'm not just a doctor. I serve other useful functions."

"You? Useful? Doing what?"

"Cookie carrier. Errand runner." He couldn't believe she was here. That Kristin, whom he'd been thinking of and trying not to think of for months, was standing in front of him. Kristin, who seemed to glow with beauty. She wore a feminine soft yellow outfit, and the quiet color made her as lustrous as the first light of dawn.

What he felt when he saw her wasn't normal. It wasn't friendship. It wasn't even that zing of interest. It was…he didn't know what it was. His soul sort of gave a hitch of recognition whenever he looked at her.

What did that mean? Why, when he'd filled his life with work and responsibility and more work, couldn't he forget her? He'd never stopped feeling sad that he'd never made that call when he was in Seattle.

No, it was for the best. He'd learned the hard way. He was terrible when it came to relationships. He wasn't good at letting people close. It wouldn't work out anyway, and look how incredible she was. So amazing. She deserved a man who could love her with all his soul.

Why was he thinking about love anyway?

He watched the wind tousle her short blond hair, ruffle those golden strands. Furrows dug into her forehead, as if she wasn't sure what to do with him. As if he was the last man she wanted to see. "Why are you doing this?"

"Mom said I had to help."

"Do you always do what your mom says?"

"If I know what's good for me." He grinned, hiking the Crock-Pot safely into the crook of his arm. "If I don't, she beats me."

"Why, hello there, Kristin." Mom came around from the driver's side, looking way too proud of herself for an innocent woman. She was pleased with her efforts to bring them together. "What a pleasure to see you again. Ryan, isn't she looking very beautiful today?"

"Yes, she is." It was only the truth.

Kristin blushed. "Thank you, Mrs. Sanders. Your new hairdo looks wonderful."

"I got it frosted. And you, young man, stop telling lies about me." As pleasant as could be, Mary thwacked him on the shoulder. "Stop it."

"See?" There was no mistaking the affection in his gaze. "Mom is only starting to forgive me for still being a bachelor."

"I want grandchildren before I die!" Mary called out as she marched along the sidewalk toward the coffee shop. "It doesn't seem too much to ask."

"I'm waiting to procreate until after I'm married." Ryan called out. "But you have a long wait. Marriage is too much to ask of a man."

Mary stormed up to the front door, too dignified to answer.

Kristin took the opportunity to take a covered casserole from the floor of the trunk. All this talk of marriage between mother and son. Had Ryan been waging the same battle with his mom as she'd been having with hers? How could her mom keep doing this to her?

"I'm so glad my mom loves me." Ryan winked as he closed the trunk. "She's in this difficult phase. I do my best with her, Lord knows."

"What phase would that be?"

"Grandchild envy. A very dangerous phase. As a doctor, I recommended counseling but she's been very rebellious. Then I told her to try pressuring Mia for a change. That's what a sister is for. To take the pressure off of me."

"It's never worked for me."

"I guess I'm doomed." He didn't feel doomed. Why was his gaze sliding upward to notice the slender curve of her calves and the sway of her lace-edged dress? The swing of her short hair and the elegant line of her back? Because she was the reason he'd decided to come home again.

He held the door for her and watched as she breezed by. She was delicate, fine boned and petite. He bet he could span her waist with his hands. Tenderness— where was it coming from?—ached hard beneath his sternum. What would it be like to hold her against his chest? To tuck her against him and shelter her—just a little—from the world?

Why was he wondering?

The coffee shop was busy as more women arrived. Some of them he recognized from his school days, some he didn't. They crowded into the room in that way women have, of talking and excitement and hugging in greeting. Gifts piled on a table against the wall, and there was Mom, waving to him from the corner, where a table just for the food was waiting.

Unfortunately Kristin was heading there, too. He followed her and still managed to keep from dropping the Crock-Pot until he delivered it safely onto the table where Mom indicated. He looked up. No Kristin. Where had she gone in the ten seconds he'd taken his eyes off her?

"Ryan." She reappeared, winding her way to him. The dress she wore was the color of pale daffodils. It made her look elegant and beautiful in a classy timeless way. She carried a stack of plates from the kitchen. She unloaded them on the table and thrust one at him. "You might as well dig in. You'll be our test guinea pig."

"If I keel over, then you know to stay away from the macaroni salad."

"Something like that."

How had he gotten more handsome? The months had rolled by, so busy with work and hoping for a new promotion, that she'd hardly been aware of the days slipping away like water. But seeing him made her aware of the time. He looked well-rested. He looked as if he'd been getting in some windsurfing time.

Not that it was any of her business. If her mom were to walk in at this exact moment and notice how she was studying the handsome doctor, think of what new levels of determination that would push her to.

She pivoted away and headed in the opposite direction. A hand on her arm stopped her.

Ryan's mom seemed to have noticed. "He could be

moving to Seattle, did he tell you? He's been hemming and hawing and this week that fancy clinic made him an offer he shouldn't pass up. I think he should take it. Don't you?"

Her brain stopped working. Odd, because the cheerful excitement in the room seemed to diminish, as if someone had turned down the volume on a radio. Whatever this was, she had to stop it right now. She had to protect her heart. She had to make sure—

A loud, excited squeal kick started Kristin's mind. She blinked, the sound crescendoed.

It was Michelle making that excited laughter. Her hand settled on her huge abdomen. "Oh! I can't believe it! I'm in labor!"

Shrieks of excitement filled the shop. Kristin stood as if transfixed as everyone jumped to life around her. Jenna, Michelle's best friend, made a call on her cell. Karen raced over and made Michelle sit down. Ryan's mom ran for her purse on the counter.

"Hey, Kristin. Don't look so shaken. She'll be all right. Promise." Ryan's hand settled against the small of her back, offering her assurance.

She believed him. How could she resist? He was everything manly and rugged and dependable. He towered over her. She should have felt dwarfed, but she felt protected. Safe. As she knew Michelle would be, too.

A strange thing happened to her heart. As he moved away, to cut through the crowd of women to kneel down at Michelle's side, it felt as if he was still at her side. Touching her. Linked to her. She felt his compassion and his care as he took Michelle's hand and leaned to whisper something in her ear.

Oh, he's wonderful. If Michelle didn't look happy enough, she lit up with more joy. Breathing deliberately, the pain seemed to pass and she relaxed. Kristin's heart filled with a floaty, airy sensation.

"Oh!" Michelle let Karen and Ryan help her to her feet. She surveyed the family and friends who had gathered just for her. "I hate to run out on, like, an awesome party. I love you all so much. But I get to go have my baby now!"

Amid cheers of excitement, Kristin stood still, riveted by the way Ryan held Michelle's arm in his. She was perfectly capable of walking to the door, but he took such care with her. Michelle, her baby sister, was all grown up, waving goodbye at the door and throwing kisses.

"Come see us in the hospital! Oh!" Her hand flew to her tummy. "You may not have to wait very long!"

"Kristin?" It was Mary, pressing something cool into her palm.

She looked down at a set of keys.

"Take my car, sweetie. It's parked the closest to the door, I think, and if you drive, then Ryan can keep watch over Michelle."

Yes, it sounded sensible. Why she felt utterly overwhelmed, Kristin couldn't say. She only knew the room silenced to her ears when it should have been loud with the din of friends' and family's excited shouts of good wishes and joy.

She moved without thought, striding into a world where the sun wasn't as bright as the sight of one man. It was as if her entire being waited until his gaze met hers. Then air rushed into her lungs and blood pumped into her heart.

When he smiled, her soul opened wide.

Chapter Thirteen

With every breath she took, it was worse. This agony of awareness beating within her spirit. It was like gazing into a too-bright light and being unable to look away. And that light was Ryan. When he spoke, his voice vibrated deep within her. When he was silent, his silence was peace in her soul.

She didn't want him there, a part of her. Affecting her. She fought as hard as she could to concentrate on driving and *only* on driving. It was impossible not to notice the man's reflection in her rearview mirror when she checked traffic. She tried to ignore him. She truly did.

But every time she breathed, she noticed the faint scent of his aftershave. It reminded her of spice and smoked wood and winter nights spent at home.

The ribbon of highway unrolled before her. The miles spun away and they were pulling off the exit in Bozeman in no time. Certainly not long enough for Michelle to finish up on her phone. She was calling everyone important, including several calls to her husband to make sure he'd be waiting for her.

And he was. As dependable as a knight of old, Brody was waiting by the entrance door. He had the car door open the moment it stopped and he took his wife's hands in his big strong ones. Their love and joy was as unmistakable as the scent of spring on the breeze. Brody slipped a protective arm around Michelle and let her lean on him, a strong rock of a man.

That was what true love looked like. The quiet gazes, the comforting touches, the deep bond that had them walking with the same stride, exchanging words without saying anything at all.

An orderly came with a wheelchair, just in time as Michelle winced in pain. Brody helped her off her feet, held her hand and they breathed together until the pain passed. Michelle relaxed, leaned her forehead to his.

"Wow." Ryan felt so close. He settled into the front passenger seat, all six feet of him. "Is that something, or what?"

"If you believe in that kind of thing."

"You don't believe in love?"

"Sure. I just don't think it lasts."

"You don't? Really? Boy, what Michelle and Brody have. That looks like forever to me." Ryan had never let anyone that close to him. He couldn't seem to remember why as he watched Brody and Michelle make their way into the hospital, hand in hand, heart to heart.

Man, it was obvious. They were deeply in love.

Wrapped up in each other, they clearly shared a deep bond. They sure made it look good. Watching them made him feel not exactly envious. He'd tried the relationship thing. He'd failed at it.

But it made him consider his possibilities. He had to consider there was the potential for that kind of link between him and Kristin.

Icy fear hardened in his veins. He shivered and pulled the door closed. No, he had to stop thinking like that. He couldn't make it work. He'd tried before and found disaster. His former fiancée had been right. He wasn't good at intimacy. He'd never let her, or any other woman he'd dated, get close enough.

So why, whenever he gazed at Kristin, did his soul stir?

He remained silent as Kristin pulled away from the curb and circled around in search of a parking spot. A couple climbing out of a new SUV waved. He recognized Kristin's older sister Kendra and her husband, who was carrying their baby daughter.

Kristin stopped and rolled down the window. "How did you two get here so quick?"

"I was loading up to come to the shower when Michelle called from Mary's car." Kendra hit her remote locks and tucked the keys in the diaper bag slung over her shoulder. "So I headed here instead of town. I hear Michelle had the best medical care on the ride over here. Thanks, Ryan."

"Hey, my pleasure. I didn't do anything. I'm an orthopedist. Good to see you again, Kendra."

"Make Kristin bring you on up. Come wait with us if you want."

Kristin glanced in the rearview. "I've got someone coming up behind me. See you inside, Sis."

She pulled into the first available space and turned off the engine. A hard pressure jammed behind her sternum. With every breath she took, it seemed to expand. She felt ready to explode. She was worried about Michelle. She was happy for Michelle. She was glad to see Kendra looking so good and content walking alongside her husband. A year ago, they were newly married. Now they were a family.

Back in Seattle tucked in her little town house with her busy life and her demanding job and errands and housework and dinner out with friends, she didn't have to think about it.

It wasn't until she was here that it hit her between the eyes like a blow. Her sisters were married and mothers. Making lives of their own. With their own families. She didn't know how they could do it, how they could risk so much.

"Kristin?"

She blinked, realizing that Ryan had circled around and opened her door. He was offering his hand like a gentleman of old. Like a man courting.

No, that couldn't be right. Ryan wasn't interested in her like that. Just as she wasn't interested in him like that. But his hand, palm up, looked so dependable and *right*. She was already moving to lay her hand on his, before she realized she hadn't meant to. It just happened. When her palm met his, his bigger fingers wrapped around, holding on. Something clicked in her heart.

A perfect fit.

Dazed, she was somehow on her feet, squinting in the vibrant spring sun. Watching him, senses spinning, as he closed the door, took the keys, pocketed them, and then moved away. She let go of him, and her hand had never felt so empty.

The wind ruffled his dark shanks of hair as he slowed his pace to match hers. "It looks like your mom just drove up. It looks like she's alone."

"Yeah. That means Dad will probably come along later." Kristin could see clearly that Mom was alone in her car. The big white sedan slowed two parking aisles over. Mom waved behind the sun-streaked glass, then drove on in her hurry to find a parking spot.

The emotion pushing against her rib cage hardened. Like a cooling ball of lead, it began to sink downward, settling into her stomach. She took a step farther away from Ryan. Their shadows traveled in front of them, and she saw them in silhouette. Two separate entities.

"Dad's busy this time of year in the fields." But that wasn't the whole truth. He and Mom hardly ever drove anywhere together, and since their two weeks in Hawaii in January, it had gotten worse. The silence between her parents was louder. The breach in their marriage painfully obvious and how sad was that?

As if he could sense her thoughts, Ryan inched closer until their shadows hovered on the blacktop side by side. "Mom mentioned that your mom is thinking about divorce."

Divorce. That word hit like an unexpected blow to her abdomen. Her mom didn't believe in divorce. Both her and Dad had to be desperately miserable to even consider such an option. She took a steadying breath.

"Oh, great. I shouldn't have said anything. You didn't know."

"No, but it's not that big of a surprise, either. It's just to hear it said out loud like that. It sounds *real*. As if there's no more hoping things might work out."

"Wow, and your parents once had a solid marriage. The best. Like my folks had, until Dad died."

"Yeah, that's the problem with love. It doesn't last. When you think about it, how can it? Life is full of hardship and disappointments and devastating loss. How can something as fragile as love survive that?"

Ryan felt something nudge his cheek, soft and silken and warm. A brief brush, and then it was gone. He looked up. The wind shivered through the old flowering cherry trees lining the parking lot, and pink blossoms fell like rain.

Kristin held out her hand, palm up, to catch the silken petals. They rained down on her, clinging to her hair, her face, her dress. Carpeting the cement at her feet.

As if heaven had overheard her and sent a sign to disagree.

The wind calmed, and the downfall stopped.

"I have these all over me. They're like little bits of

silk." She stopped, her slim skirt swishing around her thighs, to brush blossoms stuck to her clothes. Her golden hair fell forward to frame her face, revealing more blossoms there.

"Here. You have some—" He reached without thinking, moving close as if he had the right. Her hair was as soft as the pink petals he carefully separated away.

"Oh," she breathed, turning to him.

Drawing his attention to her mouth. Ryan cupped her lovely face. Cradled her delicate jaw in his hands. There was no thought. No plan. No intention. Just a feeling so strong and true, it overwhelmed him. Drove him forward. He watched her bow-shaped mouth part slightly in surprise, but it was too late. He wanted to know her warm kiss. She was like spun sugar and spring light. Hope like no other.

He brushed her lips with his.

What did he think he was doing? Kristin wanted to argue, but she didn't seem able to push him away. Instead her hands closed on his shoulders, holding on. His kiss was a storm tearing across the western sky. Like lightning crackling along the horizon.

When he broke the kiss, his hands remained a tender claim against her cheek. The sun behind him haloed him, gracing him with a rare, brilliant light.

Everything within her stilled.

Afraid to breathe, afraid to break the magic, she closed her eyes. His touch sparked like fireworks popping in a midnight sky. Bold and bright and unmistakble.

A longing, sweet and intense, knifed through her. Longing for what could never be.

She stepped away, tuning into the real world around her. The place where love was not perfect, where impatient horns blared, where her mom was hurrying, her shoes clacking on the concrete. Where a siren announced the arrival of an ambulance at the emergency entrance down the way. This was a world where love couldn't last.

"Ryan." It was her mom, hurrying up, her big black purse swinging from her forearm, her free hand holding the scarf on her head with the other. "I can never thank you enough for staying with Michelle during the drive to the hospital. I didn't worry a bit knowing you were with her."

"I was glad I could help, although I didn't do a thing. Michelle seemed to be handling everything just fine."

"That's my Michelle," Mom said fondly, sparkling. And not only at the thought of the new grandchild ready to come into the world.

No, Mom was near to bursting. She had to have witnessed the kiss. There was no way she could have missed it.

Panic set in. Kristin started walking. She needed space. She needed perspective. She needed to obliterate the memory of that fantastic, emotion-filled kiss from every neuron in her brain. Because there was no way she was going to get carried away or let her feelings spiral out of control.

She didn't need anyone. Especially not Ryan. He

made her feel way too much. And he just thought he could kiss her any time he wanted? She ought to be insulted.

She wanted to be angry. She wanted to be so consumed with fury she didn't have to think about what she'd done. About how she'd practically run into the building, dashed through the lobby and bolted into the first elevator to open, even though it was going down, because she wanted to put as much distance as she could between her and Ryan.

But she hadn't left him at all. Not really. He was right there, in her heart and in her soul. Linked.

What was she going to do about that?

Since she took the long way to the maternity floor, down to the basement and back up again, Mom was already in the family waiting area.

One quick glance told her that Ryan wasn't there. He must have gone back to his mom's car and gone home. Good. She had enough to worry about without him around.

"Kristin, come sit with me." Kendra patted the hard plastic chair next to her. On her other side, her husband, Cameron, was talking on his phone, his low mumble hardly audible above the excited conversation.

Kirby and Sam arrived, with Michael leading the way. He still carried his plastic dump truck everywhere he went, but he was bigger. Taller. A little boy with thick dark hair and big blue intelligent eyes.

"Kristin!" It seemed impossible for Kirby to look any happier, but she did. "Oh, it's so good to see you!

This is what I get for being late to the shower. I missed all the excitement, and seeing you. You look good. Tired. You're working too hard."

"Guilty, but I'm up for this cool promotion. I really want it." Love for her sisters was the kind of love a girl could count on. She hugged Kirby, careful of her growing girth. "How are mommy and babies?"

"Healthy and happy."

Kirby looked it, too. She seemed to glow from the inside out, and the joy on her face doubled when her husband took her hand to help her into a chair. "Oh, that feels better. Thanks, handsome."

"Anything for you, beautiful." Sam kissed her, the way a husband kisses his wife, and means it. That's true love.

Ryan had kissed her like that. Kristin's throat ached with too much emotion, a wild jumble of feelings that she didn't want to name and didn't want to feel. She remembered Ryan's kiss. How could she forget it? Her lips sparkled. Her soul sparkled. That's how Ryan had kissed her.

Panic shot through her and she bounced out of the chair. "I'm going to the cafeteria," she announced too fast, already striding toward the elevator. "Anybody want anything?"

"Tea," Kendra answered. "Want me to come with you?"

"No!" She wanted to be alone, but she wasn't fooling Kendra, who was watching her with concern. Or Kirby, who was gazing up over the top of her little boy's cowlick, an unasked question clear on her face.

She loved her sisters, and she knew they loved her back, but they wouldn't understand. They couldn't. They had chosen to hide from the fact that you were born into this world alone, and you left it alone. That no matter how much you loved someone, that didn't stop them from dying. Loss was a part of life she didn't want, no way. And she wasn't going to close her eyes, open her heart and love as if loss wasn't inevitable.

No. She'd been there once. Allison's death had brought Mom to her knees in despair. Broken Dad's spirit for good. And it was all Kristin could do at the time to keep going through life with the grief. Taking her exams and the SAT she'd already paid and signed up for. Cooking meals that no one would eat, because her mom couldn't. Of trying to hold on to the broken pieces of her life, her heart, her family.

It had taken years before she'd been on an even keel again, before Mom came out of her dark depression and Dad began to talk a little, even if he spent most of his time in the fields or in his workshop.

Grief took a hard toll. Kristin only had to look at her mom to see the cost. The woman who'd been so vibrant and bustling and humming everywhere she went. It was as if a light had forever died inside her.

The cafeteria wasn't crowded and she took her time making up a tray of tea and coffee for everyone. Chai tea for Kendra, chamomile for Kirby, mint for Karen. Coffee with sweeteners and black tea with honey for the brothers-in-law. She didn't know them well enough to know what they would want. For Mom she waited for the apron-clad girl behind the counter to whip up a mochaccino. It helped to do this, something normal, something useful. But she couldn't forget her thoughts completely.

The kiss. That's the way she was going to think about it forever. Her first real kiss. Wow, and she hadn't even wanted it. If only she could erase it from her memory entirely. She wished she could hit the rewind button on her life and do that one moment over when he cupped her face with his amazing hands and claimed not just her mouth, but her heart and soul. How could a simple brush of lips be everything? The past, present and future all in one moment?

Stop thinking about it. That's what she had to do. Figure out a way to blot it from her mind. *The kiss* was never going to happen again. *The kiss* was a single aberration in her life centered around quiet, sensible choices and a serious work ethic. Before *the kiss,* she was a person who balanced her checkbook, set aside savings every month, paid her mortgage before the due date and was in bed by ten every night. She wore sensible shoes and a wild night out on the town was dinner with her cousin at their favorite burger place.

And she intended to be exactly the same person after *the kiss.* It wasn't a life-changing moment. It wasn't a soul-shattering experience. It was *never* going to happen again.

Because if it did, then the power of it would shatter everything she'd spent her life building. It would unbalance her carefully ordered world. It would make her want something she could never put her faith in—love.

By the time she made it back to the waiting area, the rest of the family had arrived. Karen with her husband Zach and their daughters. Gramma was reading Allie her favorite picture book.

Allie had changed, too. She'd grown taller and willowy, the toddler softness gone. Her shoulder-length straight hair shimmered like sunlight on the finest gold. She chattered away to Gramma; having the story memorized, she took over the telling. A preschooler.

Dad appeared around the corner, leaning a bit to the left where Emily held his hand tightly as she skipped on her pink strappy sandals. A toddler now. He looked younger, happier, in the company of his granddaughter.

He spotted the drink carriers. "There's my girl. You wouldn't happen to have a black coffee in there for me?"

"The biggest one is for you, right there in the corner." Kristin balanced the eggboard carrier while her dad helped himself to the large-size cup.

Dad seemed better. He kept his distance from Mom, but at least he looked content, almost like his old self as he led Emily to the play area in the corner. Together, Granddad and granddaughter constructed a house of blocks, which Michael and his truck crashed into with appropriate sound effects.

"Kristin, see what you're missing." Gramma winked over the top of Allie's blond head. "Life without love is just existing. Life without family is like being lost on an island. Life passes a person right on by and keeps going."

She'd take the island any day.

Except right now, at this moment, as she handed out the drinks, she couldn't deny the horrible pain stabbing her directly in the heart. A pain that felt like grief. Not over her sister's death, she realized.

Grief for herself. For the life she'd lost.

She examined the life her sisters had chosen. Fragile or not, they had husbands who gazed at them as if they were the only women in the world. They had children who played and laughed and gave sweet kisses. True love, the kind that was the most fragile of all, was in this disinfectant-scented room with the hard plastic chairs and the stark cold tile floor. The love they'd brought with them. The love they held in their hearts. The love they shared for Michelle as they gathered to wait. To pray for her. To be there to celebrate the new life she was being given to love and guide and protect.

How many gatherings like this had she missed? Every single one of them. She'd missed every one of her nieces' and nephews' births. Except this one.

Ryan, he was the reason she was feeling like this. His kiss…what had it done to her?

Confused, she took the empty carriers to the garbage can in the hall, poured two packets of sugar into her chai tea and sat down to wait. She couldn't help wondering. Where was Ryan now? Was he regretting kissing her? Or had she hurt him by running away?

Two hours and eighteen minutes later, Brody appeared to announce the birth of their son. Ten-pound, eight-ounce Gabriel Peter, named after his daddy and grandfather.

Ryan watched the sunset bleed like a wound. The proud rugged peaks of the Rocky Mountain Front glowed crimson beneath a troubled sky. The hospital parking lot felt abandoned. Although it was crammed with cars, he was the only one making his way across the petal-strewn pavement.

The gusty winds had stripped all but a few petals from the trees. Dark limbs reached upward, through the haze of light from the tall structure. The first cold raindrops fell as he dashed inside.

There was no wait for an elevator in the lobby, which was nearly as quiet as the parking lot had been. As he jostled the packages and gifts for Michelle's baby, he punched the button for the maternity floor.

Kristin had been on his mind for hours. The memory of their kiss remained like a whisper in his soul. The sort of whisper that was too quiet to hear the words, no matter how hard he listened. All he knew was that it had brought him here.

All was calm as he strode down the hallway. His boots beat like his pulse down the long corridor. He followed the shine of fluorescent lights on the tile to the last door on his right. It was half open and, hidden in the shadows, he raised his knuckle to knock but froze at the sight of Kristin. She was seated in a chair, graced by the glow of a lamp, so still and calm he could see the rare and beautiful love within her as she gazed down at the tiny bundle she cradled in her arms. A newborn child.

In the space between one heartbeat and the next, he saw the world shift around him and time roll forward. For one brief moment he saw her holding a different child wrapped in a similar blue receiving blanket, dark downy hair curling beneath the blue infant cap.

His son.

In her arms.

She was his fairy tale—enchanting and kind and a vision of everything good and dear. She stole his heart and he couldn't have stopped his feet from moving forward anymore than he could have stopped his heart from beating.

He lost his heart. It was gone. No longer his.

More sure than he'd ever been in his life, he walked into the light.

Chapter Fourteen

What was this ache inside her, so sharp and fierce it was like a great pain?

She felt as if places within her spirit were being opened for the first time. Places open only to the man who emerged from the shadowed doorway, with flowers in one hand and helium balloons trailing behind. He seemed like a dream, her dream. Had she been thinking so hard about Ryan that she'd conjured him up from her imagination?

No, he was real. His step a hush on the floor, his presence as tangible as the pain in her heart. Wearing ordinary wash-faded jeans and a black T-shirt, he was manly, all right. Just watching him made the woman in her give thanks.

Strong and steadfast, he towered over her. He was all she could see. All she wanted to see. Her spirit silenced. The places within her swelled with a strange force that was like pain. But no, it wasn't pain exactly. She didn't know what it was, but when Ryan knelt before her, it brought tears to her eyes.

"Look what a precious gift you're holding." When he spoke, it was as if he tugged at strings stuck to those tender places deep within her.

An odd pulling at her heart and her soul that made her ready to shatter. She couldn't bear to look at him, it hurt so much. She gazed down at the new life cradled in the crook of her arm. Looking at her new nephew made a different place within her spirit hurt, too.

She cleared her throat before she answered, and her voice came out as a rough whisper. "This is our newest blessing from God."

Ryan leaned closer to study the sleeping infant. His eyes tightly shut. One fist visible. "It blows me away every time I see a new baby. Look at those tiny fingers. They're just so…new."

"And precious." Kristin's eyes burned, and she didn't dare disturb Gabe, who'd had a hard time drifting off to sleep. "I've got another incredible nephew. I'm a pretty lucky aunt."

"You surely are." His rumbling baritone was like a kiss to her soul.

She shivered. The pain within her, that wasn't a pain at all, became something more. An emotion she would not acknowledge. She *couldn't.*

"Michelle and Brody are just down the hall, if you want to give her those flowers."

"Down the hall? I can't imagine they'd want to leave this little guy."

"Only because I swore I wouldn't take my eyes off him. They're having dinner. It's a special thing the hospital does, serves steak-and-lobster dinner to the new parents. They have it catered. It's really nice."

"They should get some time together, because they may not have a quiet romantic dinner for some time to come."

"Exactly. That's why I volunteered to stay with him. Besides, tomorrow I head home, right after Easter dinner. I have a big day on Monday. It's work stuff. So I thought I'd get in as much baby holding as I could. Next time I see him will be, gosh, next Thanksgiving, when I come home again. He'll be seven months old. He'll be so different than this."

"Yep. Babies have a tendency to do this. Grow up."

"Yeah." The intense emotions she refused to feel became sharp enough to spike through flesh and bone, that's what it seemed like as baby Gabriel's sweet round face blurred. Everything became a fuzzy cloud as she blinked hard and fast.

What was wrong with her?

"He sure is something. I bet holding him makes you think about having one of your own one day."

"He sure is precious. Michelle and Brody are blessed to have him."

"Yeah. Aren't they?" Ryan's chest thrummed with a yearning so strong, it felt ready to blow him apart. He thought of how he'd been sitting on the back steps, feeling the night come. Missing his dad.

Seeing the past, present and future in the same moment, what was and what could be, made him sure. As if his dad was watching out for him from heaven after all. Once, Dad had been like this, gazing at the woman he loved with a newborn in her arms.

The seasons of life come full circle. He understood it now. What was the quote? There is a time for every season. As one season was linked to the next, so was one life linked to another. His father to his. And, one day, God willing, his life to his son's. Love was the glue that bonded them together for good.

This world was full of hardship and tragedy, accidents and illness, of loss, but of renewal, too. And God's great gift of love.

That's what this was in his heart, in his soul. Love, honest and true. As infinite as heaven. As precious as grace. And it filled him with tenderness so rare, it overpowered everything. Made everything clear.

All that mattered in his life was right in front of him. Kristin. Deep furrows dug into her forehead. Her eyes shimmered with unshed tears. He could feel her sadness, for his heart was hers. A life not lived was its own sorrow. He knew, because that's how he went through his days, too. Existing, and it was no way to live.

He was already reaching. His fingers already aching for the different texture of hers. He covered her hand, and the link between them strengthened. His soul sighed.

Now, all he had to do was to come up with the right words. How did he start? "I'm absolutely sure of one thing. I'm going to be moving to Seattle."

"Your mom mentioned that you were thinking about it."

"Yep. Phoenix is just too far away."

"From your mom?"

"From you."

The spikes in her rib cage lengthened. Sharpened. She felt this way because of the baby she was holding. The beloved new life asleep in her arms, trusting and innocent. Maybe it was her biological clock starting to tick.

Or maybe it was that she was afraid if she met Ryan's gaze, she would want everything she couldn't believe in. Even if she wanted it, she couldn't. Not knowing what she knew about life. About loss.

No, she wasn't going to let him go any farther. She had to hold on to her heart. She took a steadying breath although she felt as if her ribs had shattered. As if a part of her were dying, but it had to be said. "We're only friends, Ryan. You shouldn't move just to be closer to me."

"Don't you feel this between us?"

No, she should say. But the truth rang within her. *Yes.* If only he could be the one. The one man she could love for every day of her life to come.

Could he be?

All she had to do was to look into his eyes to see it. Yes. This all-consuming agony within her was love. Love for this man kneeling before her, and she couldn't let herself feel it or it would move through her like a mountain creek, refreshing and sweet, and it would tear her stable world apart.

"Excuse me." She waited for him to remove his hand

and stand so she could lay baby Gabriel in his bassinet. With her arms empty, it was easier to close her heart. To face him, even though he'd let the balloons go. They hopped along the ceiling toward the other bouquets of balloons in the corner.

He held the flowers, white lilies and pink roses, to her. "I've got to say this. I don't know if the moment is right, but I know your sister and her husband are going to be walking through that door soon. And you'll be surrounded with your family again and tomorrow, with Easter. And then you'll be gone."

"Don't, Ryan." She had to be smart about this. She had to stop him before he went too far. Her entire life depended on it. "I don't want you to say—"

"I love you."

For one split second she felt as light as the balloons he'd brought. She seemed to be floating. When Ryan took her hand, she felt dizzy and joyous and terrified all at once. As if she were falling through the stratosphere without a parachute. With only the earth far below to break her fall.

His kiss sparkled across her lips. Soft and warm and wonderful. Like a dream she wanted to hold on to as tight as she could and never let go. But how could she? She broke away from his amazing tenderness, feeling her heart buckle and her soul crack.

She'd chosen her life for a reason. Look at the baby, so infinitely precious. If she kept following this new path, it was too much to lose. Life was like that. Look at Mom and Dad. Love didn't last. Not even the best of loves. People let you down, death happened. The steel she'd found in herself, that had gotten her through her family falling apart, Allison's death and losing the parents she used to have, was strong.

Very strong. She could feel what was next as Ryan's heart opened more. He was going to propose. She could feel it. She could see his dreams as if they were her own. Married, life along the lakeshore in Seattle, children and car pools and quiet evenings after the little ones were sleep.

No! It took all her effort to take one jerky step away. To put distance firmly between them. She swore she could hear what remained of her heart crumbling into dust. "I think I hear my sister."

She felt Ryan watching her as she circled away from him. Swore she could feel his heart turning to dust, too.

Desperate, she popped into the hall and there was Michelle, hand in hand with her husband. The two of them walking slow and leisurely, moving as if one, caught up in each other. True love.

Kristin tore her gaze away. Ryan was right behind her, his hands falling to her shoulders. It was the sweetest thing, his love. His unwavering devotion.

Emotion wedged tight in her throat made it impossible to speak. Everything within her begged her to turn into Ryan's arms and reach out to him. To kiss him the way she longed to. With all the tenderness she had. With all the love stored up just for him.

"This isn't over," he whispered.

"Yes, it is." She meant it. She had to. This man would be so much to lose. Whether over time as love faded to nothing. Or from the inevitable truth that this earthly life wasn't forever. Ryan already had a piece of her soul. Losing him would be losing *everything*.

How could she put her faith in that? She couldn't do it. No. She stepped out of his touch, turned away and gave thanks when Michelle and Brody arrived in the room, chasing away the tension, bringing their joy.

Kristin left the moment she could and was grateful when she stepped out into the night. Alone, she raced the first raindrops to her mom's car and collapsed into the driver's seat. While the defroster chugged away at the foggy window, she watched Ryan emerge from the building and disappear into the black curtain of cold rain, taking her heart with him.

She was one raw nerve by the time she reached her parent's house. Wrung out and soul weary, she didn't care that she was drenched to the skin on the walk between the detached garage and the house. The world around her was as pitch-black as hopelessness, but the light from the kitchen window glowed, drawing her gaze.

Easter decorations were everywhere. From the basket of candy eggs on the counter to the colorful clings in the window, to the cross as the centerpiece on the table where Mom was standing. She had Emily at her side, kneeling on a chair, their heads bent together decorating sugar cookies.

"Pink! Pink!" Emily was chanting as Kristin opened the door.

"Yes, you did a good job with the pink buttons. Now, let me give our bunnies happy smiles. See?" Mom patiently squeezed frosting onto cutout cookies laid out in neat rows on a cookie sheet. "Oh, Kristin. There you are. Ryan called looking for you. I tacked his cell number up on the bulletin board."

This isn't over, he'd told her. He was certainly a man of his word. Too tired, feeling half-dead inside, she dropped her keys on the counter. She'd deal with Ryan later. What she wanted more than anything was to lie down. Maybe she'd take a book and a cup of tea and—

The oven timer beeped. She reached over to turn it off.

"Kristin, honey, could you take the loaves out for me. I've got my hands full. If you don't mind?"

"Loaves? Of bread? What are you doing baking bread at this hour?"

"Tomorrow's going to be a busy day. With everyone coming for Easter dinner, and Michelle coming home in the evening, and her house to get ready, and all the cooking." Mom set aside the tube of frosting. "Emily and I sure have been busy."

"Yum," Emily agreed, licking the finger she'd swept through the bowl of colored sugar. She was adorable and she knew it. She wiped her hands on her ruffle-edge pink shirt and grinned like the princess she was.

"And you!" Mom's chuckle was thin edged, but there was no mistaking the joy she took in being with one of her granddaughters. "What color should we make the bunnies' shirts?"

"Yum!" Emily answered with glee, reaching for a second helping to the sugar topping.

Too cute. Kristin grabbed the oven mitts and took the first loaf from the oven. She popped the golden loaf from the pan and flipped it onto the cooling rack. The second loaf stuck and she shook gently, waiting for it to release.

That's when she noticed the bottle of antacid on the counter. It was safely out of Emily's reach, but hadn't been put back in the cupboard. One thing Mom never did was leave clutter anywhere, even one bottle. She really *must* be tired.

And it was Kristin's fault. Instead of coming right home from the hospital, she'd driven around in the rain and lightning for hours until her emotions had settled into a quiet wooden numbness. That wasn't good, either, but it was better than feeling as if she'd been broken wide open from the inside out.

If she'd come straight home, then she would have been able to help Mom.

The loaf tumbled into her protected hand, and she turned the bread over to cool. She'd left a dent in the top and she patted at it, hoping it would go back into its original shape.

"That's all right, honey." Mom sounded tired as she circled around the island. "Can you keep an eye on Emily for me?"

"Sure. I haven't lost my touch at decorating cookies."

"That sure would be a help. The potatoes should be chilled long enough, and if I whip up the salad now, it would be one less thing to do tomorrow morning." Mom hefted the big bowl of diced potatoes from the refrigerator shelf and winced. Her hand flew to her chest. "Goodness, my stomach's acting up again."

"You do too much, and you keep everything inside. Just like me." Kristin took the bowl from her mom and glanced over to check on Emily, who'd helped herself to a handful of M&M's and was eating them one at a time by color. She handed the bottle of antacid to her mother. "Take a few, and then let me make you a cup of tea. You rest, I'll finish up here."

"What about Emily?"

"She can help me, right, Emily?"

Emily's mouth was too full of chocolate to answer, but she looked agreeable enough.

"See? We're more than capable." Kristin's stomach took a tumble. Mom was really pale. And the bruised circles beneath her eyes told of her stress. While she'd refused to talk about what happened in Hawaii and what happened between her and Dad since, she clearly wasn't sleeping well.

"Go upstairs, that's an order. I'll bring you up a cup of tea as soon as it's ready."

"But the potato salad—"

"I'll follow the recipe. I have a college degree. I know how to read." Gently, she kissed her mom's ashen cheek. "Please."

A knock thundered at the back door.

"Who'z it?" Emily hopped off the chair.

"I'll get Emily *and* answer the door. Sit down." Kristin knew who was standing on the other side of the door. Even if she couldn't see him through the glass panes, she could feel his presence and his determination.

The little girl stood on tiptoe, using both hands, but she wasn't quite tall enough to turn the knob. With one swoop, Kristin hefted the toddler onto her hip and opened the door.

He stood there, as dark as the night, soaking wet. "We have to talk. I want to finish this. I need to."

"Now's not a good time." She glanced at her mom, who had sunk into one of the breakfast bar chairs. Her head was in her hands. "Mom?"

"Oh, I'm just not feeling well. I'm tired, that's all." Mom's voice came thin and breathy. A few beads of sweat clung above her upper lip. "I just, oh, need to go lie down, I guess."

"What is it, Mrs. McKaslin?" Ryan was at her side in a second, his jaw tense, his gaze concerned. "Been working too hard, huh? What seems to be the trouble?"

"Upset stomach. I took some of these tablets my doctor recommended."

"How long ago?" Ryan sounded casual, calm.

He wasn't. Kristin could feel his tension. She closed the door, afraid to move as Ryan gently took Mom's hand in his and felt her wrist. Waited as he timed her pulse.

"Any dizziness? Does your jaw hurt? Or your neck?"

"My neck. It's nothing, just my stomach, you know how pain travels."

"Yes, I do. Kristin, get me a bottle of aspirin, would you? And call for an ambulance." He could have been asking for a cup of tea, he didn't seem alarmed at all. But when his gaze met hers, she knew that he was.

Something was wrong with her mother. Keeping a tight hold on Emily, she rummaged through the cupboard, knocking aside vitamin containers until she found the aspirin. She tossed it across the counter to him, reached for the phone and hit the numbers without thinking. As she anxiously waited for the county dispatch to pick up, it seemed to be an eternity between the first ring and the second.

"Just lie right here on the floor, that's right."

"Goodness, there's just nothing wrong that a good night's sleep won't cure." Mom argued, even as Ryan helped her to the floor. "Oh, I *do* feel weak."

"That's because you're probably having a mild heart attack. At the very least an angina attack. Just relax. I'm here. I'll take care of you."

"What a good man you grew up to be," Mom said shakily as she placed her hand on Ryan's big capable one. "It's my stomach. There's no need to fuss."

"Just humor me." Ryan's kindness shone like a rare light.

"Hello—9-1-1. What is your emergency, please?" came a woman's capable voice across the line.

It was a blur, time taking on a strange slowness as she verified the address, and held the line as Ryan held

Mom's wrist, keeping track of her pulse, keeping her calm. Ready and vigilant.

Where was Dad? Why wasn't he in the house at this time of the evening? Kristin couldn't hang up to try the outside shop or barn lines. She could only wait until the ambulance arrived and the medics poured into the house, with their equipment and their gurney and their squawking radios. Emily started to cry at the noise, and trying to comfort her, Kristin made a few quick calls. No answer. Where was he? What if Mom…*died?*

No, she couldn't think about that. Or how pale and weak Mom looked, surrounded by men and monitors as they rushed her out of the house and into the night. Lights flashed, cutting through the rain as the firemen and paramedics took her mom away.

Praying as she went, Kristin turned off the ovens, grabbed the car keys and Emily's diaper bag. She was shaking so hard, she couldn't get Emily's coat zipped, so she left it, huddling the little girl against her for warmth.

Her sisters. She had to call her sisters. Trembling, she took a steady breath, wiped the rain out of her face, and saw Ryan. He was in the back of the ambulance, his gaze like a force that drew her.

Without a word, she *knew*. She could count on him to do his best for her mom. She knew, too, as lightning raced across the sky, that she wasn't alone. God was watching over all of them on this dark, hopeless night.

Easter Sunday

The McKaslin family gathered in the ICU waiting area. Ryan wasn't surprised to see everyone there but Kirby, who'd stayed behind to keep watch over the children. Only the adults were there—the sisters and their husbands, the grandmother and grandfather, in various states of dress. Those who had been pulled out of their beds wore pajamas underneath their coats.

The oldest sister, Karen, still wearing the fuzzy slippers she'd received Kristin's call in, spotted him first. She clung to her husband's steadying hand, fear stark on her face.

Kristin, holding a sleeping Emily, rose quietly, careful not to waken the child in her arms. It was a sweet sight. Ryan's hopes warmed. Yeah, he had hope. Because there was only one outcome to this. And he was going to do whatever it took to make it right between him and Kristin.

"We haven't heard anything." She kept her voice a low whisper. "No one's said anything. Dad is trying to get some answers, but he's not back yet."

"I saw him. He's talking to the doctor, who should be out to talk to you all shortly. She's all right."

Relief shuddered through her. He felt it, just as he could feel her pain. And her love. "It's because of you. You were there. You knew what to do."

"I'm handy to have around. I was hoping you might have noticed that by now." Gently, because now wasn't the time, he ran his hand over her hair. He'd never seen her look so disheveled. Her hair was tangled and had dried however the wind had last left it. Her mascara was smeared away and her eyes were red from tears.

He'd never loved her more.

"Just relax, okay?" He inched close enough to rest her cheek on his chest, loving the way she leaned against him.

It was sweet, holding her. And Emily, too, sleeping so soundly. He just opened his heart to the moment. To Kristin. And he felt the love inside, intense and brilliant and overwhelming.

Love of a brighter hue than he'd ever imagined. So radiant, his soul ached with the power of it.

As if she felt it, too, her fingers curled into his shirt. She held on to him as if she never wanted to let go.

Chapter Fifteen

Every minute that had passed since she'd pushed away from Ryan's arms was torture. And it had only worsened after Zach offered to take Emily with him to drop her off with Kirby who was watching all the children. At least when she'd had Emily to hold, she had someone to think about besides Ryan. But the little girl was probably tucked in for the rest of the night, and Kristin wished she could feel as safe and insulated.

Mom's condition could worsen. She could die. And then what? Just thinking of that possibility for half of a nanosecond brought suffocating black pain that made it hard to breathe. Would she lose Mom, too?

Sitting on the edge of the hard plastic chair, Kristin swiped the wetness from her eyes. *No, don't even think like that. Mom is going to make it.* She'd had a mild heart attack, and the doctor who'd been treating her came out to assure them she was stable. They were very pleased how well she'd responded to their treatment.

What if their prayers and the doctors' care weren't

enough? What if she had another attack? A thousand horrible possibilities flashed through her mind. Frightening scenarios. She *so* wanted to slide into the vacant chair next to Ryan, lean her head on his shoulder and soak in the comfort of his strong arms tightening around her. Shivering with panic, she couldn't sit still for another minute. She was terrified a doctor was going to come around the corner and tell them that Mom was gone.

She darted past Ryan and kept on going. She could feel his questions—why was she going, where was she going, why hadn't she turned to him? Although his gaze was like a magnet pulling her back, she didn't stop until she was safely around the corner and out of his sight. Then she slumped against the wall, the faint beep of monitors echoing down the sterile corridor.

Had Ryan felt the same shifting in his soul when they kissed? The same harmony when he held her? The link between their souls? She wanted to stay in his arms forever. With everything inside her, she fought to stay where she was instead of running around the corner to him. To know the sweet perfection of holding him.

She'd done it once. Twice would be too scary to think about.

A prickle of awareness flitted through her, and she heard the pad of his boots coming closer. He was coming after her. She was way too vulnerable, her every nerve exposed. Panic had her zooming down the hall before he could find her. Afraid because she yearned for this man with all the deepest parts of her soul.

She whipped around a second corner, knowing all

she'd done was buy herself time. She had to deal with wonderful, tender, incredible Ryan. There could never be a future for them. No way—

She skidded to a halt on the tile floor. The sight of a lone man sitting on a chair jerked her out of her thoughts. He sat with his elbows on his knees, his face in his hands, his fingers anxiously combing through military-short graying hair. The man looked so grief-stricken as he lifted his head to swipe at his eyes. Tears stained his cheeks. Blind in his sorrow, he lowered his face again. He was wearing a flannel blue-plaid shirt and old jeans with a rip at the hem.

"Dad?" Fear racked through her. Shaking, she made her wooden, quaking legs carry her to the man's side.

The man who looked so alone. When he looked up at her, there was no light in his blue eyes. There were only the shadows and dull darkness of a man who had lost everything.

Mom's dead. That was the only thing that would make Daddy look like that. Kristin knew, sinking to the floor, remembering the last time she'd seen him like this when Allison died.

Had they lost Mom, too? The tile was cold, the over-head fluorescent lighting a bright surreal shine that blurred as tears roared upward with the pain of complete loss.

"Oh, Kris." Dad's deep voice broke. "They said I should g-go on in and sit with her. She needs me to c-comfort her."

Comfort her? Hot tears scorched her throat and

burned her eyes as relief took the last of her strength. Mom was alive. She was okay. *Thank you, Lord.* She still had her mother.

But not her father. Her dad was breaking apart. Pinching the bridge of his nose to hold back the wetness pooling in his eyes.

"I can't go in there." Dad's mouth trembled. Fighting to hold everything in. "I thought when I buried Allison, that's it. I just can't take any more. It killed me, I tell you. It killed your mother, too. She kept trying to hold on to me, and I just kept moving back. I know she needed me, you girls needed me. But I loved you all so much. I couldn't take any more."

"Oh, Daddy." Kristin's heart broke although it was in pieces already. She gazed at her quiet father who'd felt so deeply but had kept it bottled up inside for so long.

"I don't think I thought it all out, but I know this for sure. I couldn't take another loss like that. The Good Lord had his reasons for taking Allison home. She was so good and pure, like every one of our girls. Why wouldn't He love her so much, He wanted her with Him? But I was just a dead man walkin'. Walkin' and workin', and barely gettin' by. And I thought, this is what comes from loving. So I guess I just stepped away. Figured it was the best way."

"I understand, Dad."

"I thought you would. You're like me in a lot of ways, Krissie. But listen to me. I'm sitting here choking on my own sorrow. I kept safe, that's what I did, and the grief is just the same. Only this time around, I see the truth. I've got nothing but regret. All that time I wasted. For the years I could have loved that woman and was too darn afraid. Now, all I've got is the same killing grief and no love in between."

"Oh, Dad." Kristin laid her hand on his. He was cold and trembling, his pain etched deeply on his face. "Just go in and sit with her."

Dad struggled to blink back his tears. "It didn't stop me from this hurtin'. I didn't wind up loving that woman any less. But it did stop me from living life with her.

"Don't make my mistake, baby girl. That man there—" Dad nodded toward the end of the hallway. "He's come with his love to offer you. You can't stop life from happening, it happens just the same. But take what care you can with these fragile blessings God has given you. Love with all your heart. It's all there is. It's everything that matters."

"Okay, Daddy." Kristin wrapped her arms around her middle. The knot of tears wedged in her throat broke apart. She hung her head as her father stood and walked away. But he was really walking toward something. To Mom. To life. To true love.

Kristin closed her eyes. Laid her face in her hands. Every part of her hurt. Daddy was right. She knew he was. But how could she risk it? There was so much to lose

So much to have, if she could reach out.

Ryan. She felt him draw nearer, for her soul turned

like a season, like the ice of winter cracking away to expose the tender new earth beneath.

Her tender, fragile heart ached from the brightness, but she turned toward the light, toward Ryan's love. He came to her and gathered her to his chest. It was like coming home to stay forever after a painful eternity spent in the cold. What would it be like to be held by him forever?

"He's a wise man, your father." Ryan's lips brushed her forehead. "I think you should take his advice."

"And love you with my whole heart?"

"As I will love you for the rest of my life. And beyond." His kiss was perfection. A promise of commitment and honor and quiet evenings spent beside him. Of love through good times and hardship. "You are my everything. That's what this is between us, this bond, this down-to-the-soul love. Will you marry me?"

It was there, his endless love for her, in his eyes, in his touch, in his dreams. She lost her heart. It was gone. No longer hers. "Yes, I want to marry you. I love you so much."

When he claimed her lips with his, she saw the fragile blessings yet to come. She saw their future. Their God-given love was like the joy of a warm spring day. Ever blooming and ever precious. Strong enough for this life and ever after.

"C'mon. Let's go check on your mom." Ryan helped her stand, wiping her tears with this thumb.

They walked away hand in hand.

Epilogue

Christmas Day, two years later

"Kristin!" Gramma called from the kitchen door. "We're waiting for you, honey. The girls have the game board all set up and ready to play in the dining room. Come and bring the cookies with you."

"Sure." The last snap fastened, she smiled down at her freshly diapered son. Matthew, two weeks old, scrunched up his face, the same way his daddy did before he yawned hugely. "Nap time for you, little one."

"I'll take him in with me." Ryan's hand settled on her shoulder.

Together they gazed down at their baby. His dark hair was Ryan's. He had eyes so blue, Kristin knew they would deepen into her family's trademark violet-blue.

"I don't think it's ever too early to expose him to football."

"Football? That's not nearly as important as starting him out young playing Monopoly. Maybe I'd better take him in with me."

She loved that she made her husband chuckle, low in his throat. He rewarded her with a tender kiss. Her soul moved, as it always did. As it always would.

"No way, babe. The third quarter is about to start, and I don't want him to miss the kickoff." With care, he scooped his son into his big protective arms. Love for Matthew shone deep in his eyes, as did his love for her.

The love she valued more than anything, for it had changed her life. Changed her.

"Kristin!" Michelle stood in the doorway this time, her new baby, Brittany, in her arms. "We're waiting!"

"Okay." She brushed a kiss on her son's forehead, so sweet and soft and perfect. Pure love lifted her up as she watched her husband and son head off for the exciting second half of the game.

"Excuse me, Aunt Kristin." Allie, in grade school now, held up one end of a blanket. "Are you done? Cuz I gotta finish makin' our tent."

"Sure." She hefted the diaper bag out of the way as the slim little girl who looked so very much like their dear sister Allison, studiously secured the end of the blanket, successfully finishing the huge tent beneath the wide round oak table.

"Okay, everyone, it's all done!" Allie flipped the edge up that was to serve as the door, and children came running. Michael, a tall sturdy preschooler, abandoned his racecar track. Hauling their baby dolls, Emily and Anna were the first to crawl into the tent.

Kristin stepped around Kirby's twins, both little girls struggling to push the same toy vacuum cleaner around the kitchen. Too cute. She snatched the cookie tray from the counter, sidestepped Gabriel, who was happy throwing his Play-Doh on the floor and at the twins, who stopped vacuuming to throw it right back.

The football game blared in the living room as the men gathered around the big screen, shouting encouragement and advice and reprimanding the refs. Mom sat next to Dad, contentedly crocheting on her latest afghan. Their love renewed.

Ryan must have felt her presence because he turned from the game, their new baby drowsing against his wide chest. Their gazes met and the link between them, soul to soul, brightened. "I love you," he whispered.

"I love you back."

"Kristin." It was Karen this time come to steal the cookies away. The pictures on the wall caught her attention. She nodded toward them. "Look. Mom has your little Matthew's picture framed and up already. There are a lot of us now."

"Yeah." Kristin noticed the pictures that were missing, but the past couldn't be changed. Only laid to rest. And her love for Allison didn't have to stop. "She's watching over us, don't you think? At least checking in to see how we're doing."

"I'm sure. We'll see her again one day, you know. That's why it's called heaven."

Kristin swallowed hard to hold back the tears. The sounds of family, of laughter and playing children and the groan of the men at an unfortunate interception rose and fell. The tides of life, of homecoming, of all that was important in this world rushed through her.

The room shifted, and it was memory she saw. Grade-school girls crowding around the dining-room table, baby Michelle toddling after them, cookie crumbs everywhere as they hurried to start the Monopoly game Santa had brought them for Christmas. In the next moment teenage girls, laughing and disagreeing just to disagree as properties were traded and money lost.

The past dissolved, leaving the present. Kirby and Michelle setting up the game. Kendra, expecting her second daughter next month, sorted through the tokens and lined up all of their usual ones on the Go square. Karen joined them, trying to distract Kirby by offering her a cookie, so she could try to grab the bank's money.

"Hey!" Kirby protested good-naturedly. "No fair. I get to be banker this time. Mom!"

"Girls, girls!" Mom scolded from the couch. "Don't make me come over there."

"*I'll* be good." With a wink, Karen successfully stole the box with the money in it. "Just tell Kirby it's *my* turn."

The old disagreement had them all laughing. Some

traditions were more treasured for all the ways they stayed the same.

There was nothing like coming home. Kristin swiped the tears from her eyes, took her place at the table and rolled the dice.

* * * * *

*Now that the McKaslin sisters have all found
true happiness it's time for their
cherished cousins to meet their soul mates.
Watch for SWEET BLESSINGS,
the next book in*
THE McKASLIN CLAN,
*on sale April 2005.
You won't want to miss this heart-stirring
Love Inspired novel about
love lost...and found again.*

Dear Reader,

All of her four sisters have discovered true love, and now it's Kristin's turn. I hope that you will be reminded, through this story, of how truly precious God's blessings are. That this earthly life may not be an easy one, but it is a beautiful gift. But Kristin's is not the final McKaslin story! The McKaslin cousins are about to find their happily-ever-afters. In April 2005, please watch for Amy's story, *Sweet Blessings*, which shows how real love happens, even when a person has given up all hope.

I wish you the sweetest of all blessings,

Jillian Hart

Take 2 inspirational love stories FREE!

PLUS get a FREE surprise gift!

Mail to Steeple Hill Reader Service™

In U.S.
3010 Walden Ave.
P.O. Box 1867
Buffalo, NY 14240-1867

In Canada
P.O. Box 609
Fort Erie, Ontario
L2A 5X3

YES! Please send me 2 free Love Inspired® novels and my free surprise gift. After receiving them, if I don't wish to receive anymore, I can return the shipping statement marked cancel. If I don't cancel, I will receive 4 brand-new novels every month, before they're available in stores! Bill me at the low price of $4.24 each in the U.S. and $4.74 each in Canada, plus 25¢ shipping and handling and applicable sales tax, if any*. That's the complete price and a savings of over 10% off the cover prices—quite a bargain! I understand that accepting the books and gift places me under no obligation ever to buy any books. I can always return a shipment and cancel at any time. Even if I never buy another book from Steeple Hill, the 2 free books and the surprise gift are mine to keep forever.

113 IDN DZ9M
313 IDN DZ9N

Name _____ (PLEASE PRINT)

Address _____ Apt. No.

City _____ State/Prov. _____ Zip/Postal Code

Not valid to current Love Inspired® subscribers.

Want to try two free books from another series?
Call 1-800-873-8635 or visit www.morefreebooks.com.

* Terms and prices are subject to change without notice. Sales tax applicable in New York. Canadian residents will be charged applicable provincial taxes and GST. All orders subject to approval. Offer limited to one per household.

® are registered trademarks owned and used by the trademark owner and or its licensee.

INTLI04R

©2004 Steeple Hill